FINAL

DEATH

Book Three in the Transhuman Chronicles

By Rose Garcia

FINAL DEATH
Book Three in the Transhuman Chronicles

Copyright © 2015 by Rose Garcia

Published by Rose Garcia Books

Cover Design by Steven Novak: Novak Illustration
Interior formatting and design by Amy Eye:
The Eyes for Editing

ISBN-13: 978-1511850674
ISBN-10: 1511850671

Other books by Rose Garcia

THE TRANSHUMAN CHRONICLES

Final Life, Book One
Final Stand, Book Two
Final Death, Book Three

ACKNOWLEDGMENTS

A trilogy... who would've thought... Honestly, I didn't know if I had it in me, but there are those out there who never doubted me—my husband, my kids, my Garcia family, my Moriarty family, my friends, and my fans. And guess what, you guys were right! Thank you for believing in me!

A very special thanks to my amazing critique partner: Heather Elliot Neill; my awesome beta readers: Mariela Bustos, Adalinda Gonzales, Jessica Ramirez, and Wade Moriarty; my kick butt Rebels street team members active at the time of printing: Mariela Bustos, Adalinda Gonzales, Jessica Ramirez, Charilene Lucas, Gabbs Warner, Jamie Jones, Sarah Lowrey, Shawna Stringer, Vanessa Strickler, Jamie Taliaferro, Hermelinda Gonzales, Ashley Pasco, Bridget Clark, Crystal Cantu, Judith Frazee, Lisa Grissinger, Samantha Wallace, Nicole Counts, Kristen Bauer, Heather Leah, Diana Cardonita, Chelsea Gromaski, and Terrie Arasin. (I apologize right now if I forgot anyone!)

A special shout-out to fellow authors Eva Pohler, Venessa Kimball, Rachel Harris, Mary Ting, Jennifer Miller, Angela Corbett, and Charyse Allan. Thanks for your help, support, and wisdom!

To the industry professionals in my life: Damaris Cardinali and Amanda Vaughn of Good Choice Reading,

Steven Novak of Novak Illustrations, Amy Eye of the Eyes for Editing, Jolinda Bivens of Swagalicious Promotional Products, and Vanessa Strickler — you guys rock!

To the people who have read my books and written reviews at various media outlets and review sites, THANK YOU SO MUCH! I appreciate you more than you know! To stay in touch regarding my appearances and future releases, please subscribe to my newsletter at www.rosegarciabooks.com/download-finallife. You'll also be able to access some deleted scenes from *Final Life* when you sign up! And for those active on social media, you can find all my social media links at the bottom of each page of my website www.rosegarciabooks.com. I'd love to stay in touch!

For all the people who thought I could do it.
You were right.

Chapter One

~ Trent ~

I always knew my life would end in tragedy. My parents were killed in a car crash. My grandfather died from cancer when I was little. My grandmother, who could "sense" things, had never mentioned anything negative about my fate, but something in her sad eyes always told me I was destined for doom.

And now, standing in my church in 1930's Houston, my great-grandmother's warning that I wouldn't make it back to my proper time ringing in my ears, I remembered something that happened to me when I was thirteen.

It was a hot Houston summer day, one hundred degrees and climbing. My *abuela* had gone to church and I had promised to work on the yard. I had every intention of mowing the grass when a group of friends came by on their bikes and asked if I wanted to go with them to the nearby palm reader's house. For years my friends and I had wanted to ding-dong-ditch over there, but we had always chickened out. Surely a quick visit in the middle of a summer day wouldn't be scary.

Or so I thought at the time.

With enough excitement and energy to drown out

any logical thinking, we pedaled down the sidewalk of Fairland Drive, a busy road filled with cars, trucks, and eighteen-wheelers zooming up and down as if competing in the Grand Prix. Most businesses facing the street were gas stations and car mechanics, though every now and again you'd find a local *taqueria*. Amidst all the commercialism stood a one-story, bright yellow, wood-paneled house with a wide, circular concrete driveway. The home stuck out like a sore thumb, complete with a billboard in the front yard that read "Curandera" and a blinking red and black sign in the window of a deck of cards with the word "Advisor" at the top.

My friends and I dared each other the entire ten-minute ride over on who would ring the doorbell, only to find the house had two entrances—one to the right and one to the left. Closer inspection revealed mounted security cameras over each door frame, both aimed directly at us. Drenched in sweat and overcome with panic, I wondered if someone inside was watching us. I turned to my friends, ready to tell them we should leave, when a voice hollered, "Hey! *Chicos!* Get out of here!"

My friends hopped on their bikes and hauled out of there while I remained frozen, curious to see the infamous *curandera* who had scared me and my friends for years. I turned back around to face the house and there, at the door to the right, stood a tall, thin, dark-skinned woman, the age of most of my friends' moms. She wore a long, black skirt and a tight shirt with the letters MK in big, gold print—definitely not the crooked-nosed witch I had envisioned.

She narrowed her eyes at me. "Are you here for a reading?" A thick, Spanish accent laced her words. For a second there, I thought of answering in her native tongue, but quickly decided against it. I didn't want her to think I was mocking her.

Determined not to let on how scared out of my mind I was, I gave a quick nod. "Yes, ma'am."

"Do you have money?"

My grandmother had taught me to always have money in case of an emergency. I patted my jeans pocket, feeling for the crumpled ten dollar bill I had shoved in there before leaving my house. "Yes, ma'am."

She held the door open and waved me over. "Come on, then."

"Trent!" One of my friends yelled out over the whooshing of passing vehicles. "Run!"

The warning call fell short as I moved to the door and into a small room. The white-painted walls reminded me of a doctor's waiting room, complete with two chairs and a table in the middle. On the wall hung a black sign with white, plastic letters listing the services offered and their prices. Without making eye contact with me, the woman pointed at the sign and began reading out loud, but only a few words stayed with me—cards, crystals, palms—and none of it made any sense. When she waited for my response, I held out my folded up money.

"I only have ten dollars."

She snatched the paper out of my hand and then opened another door right behind her, which I hadn't noticed. "I can do a mini-reading for ten."

I followed her into another white-walled room that looked like an office. The odor of incense that smelled like Sunday mass flooded my nostrils and made my head swim. I even thought the floor tilted a little, like a creepy fun house you find at carnivals.

The woman made her way to the other side of a desk with a smooth, white top and sat in a big, black chair. I took a seat across from her and waited while I glanced over rocks, candles, and a framed picture of Jesus. My gaze settled on the bearded face. My mind imagined the Son of God telling me to get up and leave, but I couldn't. I didn't want to be a coward.

The *curandera* scooped up a cluster of crystals, some dull, others sparkly, and moved them from hand to hand. A thin, red chord was tied around her wrist. "For ten dollars, I can tell you a little of your past, your present, and your future." She talked loud and fast, keeping her eyes on her hands. "If you want to know more, you can come back, but you'll need more money. Understand?"

"Yes, ma'am."

"And you cannot tell anyone what I have said to you. If you do, it will bring you bad luck. Understand?"

"Okay," I said in a half-whisper, suddenly overcome with guilt for leaving my house without telling my *abuela*, and scared to death of the witch's warning.

"Take these stones and hold them," she said, holding her hand out to me but still not making eye contact.

I wiped my sweaty palms on my jeans, took the rocks, and held them tight. They were cold and smooth, like little eggs pulled right out of a refrigerator.

The woman opened her desk drawer and brought out a deck of cards. She shuffled them and laid out a single row. The cards were brown with pictures of men who looked like knights and ladies in long robes.

The woman eyed the cards with a frown, her hands hovering over them nervously. She grunted with annoyance, then scooped them back up into the deck. After another shuffle, she laid out a fresh row, and for the first time since I entered her presence, she stared directly at me. Her heavily lined eyes seemed like pools of dark knowledge—knowledge I suddenly knew should make me afraid. Chills swept across my skin.

"What is this?" she muttered to me before returning her gaze to the cards, as if accusing me of something.

My stomach dropped. The stones in my hand started to warm. I scooted to the edge of my chair and peered at the cards. "What?"

"You are everywhere," she whispered, "and nowhere."

My chest tightened and I knew I needed to get out of there. I pushed my seat back. The legs of the chair screeched over the marble floor. "I should—"

"No!" she commanded. "You cannot leave!"

She picked up the cards in front of me, set them aside, and laid out a third row. I eyed the images and immediately spotted a card in the middle with a knight on a horse holding a black flag with a skull on it. At the bottom of the card was the word "Death." She snapped up the card and held it to her chest. She stared me down as if I were some sort of devil.

"Get out! ¡*Vete de aqui*!" She jumped to her feet and threw the ten dollar bill at me. "Now!"

The burning rocks spilled out of my hands as I spun around, charging out of there as if my life depended on it.

***

"Hey, Trent. Back to the cabin," Farrell said, pulling me from my memory of the *curandera* and returning me to St. Joseph's church in 1930. The look of focus and determination on his face told me he believed I could take us back to the Boardman, the place from which we had time jumped, even if I didn't completely believe it myself.

Dominique, Infiniti, and Farrell moved into a circle. "Yeah, the cabin," I said, locking hands with Dominique on one side and Infiniti on the other. Fleet, who was really

Dominique's traitor dad in disguise, took his place across from me and in between Infiniti and Farrell.

Dominique sneaked a quick glance my way. She tried to give me a reassuring smile, but her eyes revealed fear, as if she knew this time jump might kill me. And even though I felt the same way, I had to cast aside my doubt and do everything I could to get us back to our own time. I couldn't let premonition rule me. But the fortune teller's look of terror as she clutched the death card haunted me.

Get it together, *man.*

I blew out, tightened my grip around Dominique's and Infiniti's hands, and forced my mind to clear as I thought of the place we were before we time-traveled, the place we needed to get back to. I pictured the Boardman River in Michigan, the tall and naked trees, the snow underneath my feet, the attack by the Tainted. And then the death card. *No!* I screamed inside my head. *Not the card,* I pleaded to myself, struggling not to think of my encounter with the *curandera* on Fairland Drive, but suddenly unable to think of anything else.

I forced my mind to obey my commands. The Boardman, the cold, the snow, the attack, I repeated over and over in my head so fast I left no room to think of anything else. I kept my face down, willing myself to get us back home, when I felt a warm glow all around me, as if someone had turned on a giant heat lamp overhead.

The Boardman, the cold, the snow, the attack.

My fingers tingled. My skin prickled with electricity. I cracked open my eyelids and saw a glowing blue hue all around me. My aura! I had never been able to see it before!

"Hey," the fake Fleet said, "what's—?"

I clamped my eyes shut again and blocked him out, pushing all my thoughts to the Boardman, when I heard the church door fling open and bang against the wall.

"No one is allowed in the sanctuary at night!" the Mother Superior called out in her gruff voice.

"You devils!" shouted the young nun who sounded and looked like my old girlfriend Veronica.

I glanced over my shoulder, remembering how the Veronica look-alike had charged Dominique with a butcher knife the first time we were here, praying I could make us time jump before she got too close.

The Boardman, the cold, the snow, the attack. The death card.

"Shit," I said out loud, trying my hardest to push those cards out of my head when the young nun pulled out a pistol. Dominique shot a look of terror my way.

This was it.

The cards.

The premonition.

They were coming true.

But damn it if I wouldn't at least send my friends back to where they belonged. I was a special Transhuman, a Supreme, and even though I didn't know what that meant, I knew I could send them back home. *Really* knew.

The Boardman, the cold, the snow, the attack.

The nun aimed the long barrel at Dominique. With the cabin finally pictured perfectly in my head and my entire body so electrified I could star in my own superhero movie, I broke the circle and lunged in front of Dominique. A popping sound like a firecracker filled the air. A heavy blow crushed my chest, followed by a sensation like a red hot poker stabbing my back.

My body crashed to the floor and slammed against the cold surface.

"Trent!"

I craned my neck and saw multicolored swirling

under Dominique and the others in a whirlpool of dust and light. Blood had splattered Dominique's face and white shirt, and I knew the crimson streaks were from me.

"Trent!" she called again, reaching out for me. Farrell held her back by her shoulders, and in a flash, they slipped from view, the ground opening and swallowing them whole.

Sirens howled in the distance. Mother Superior and the young nun rushed at the now-empty spot, circling around and looking for the four bodies that had stood there moments earlier.

"Where did they go?" Mother Superior asked out loud as if God himself could answer her somehow. Her voice echoed all around, bouncing off the concrete pillars and marble floor.

Hot, sticky wetness covered my chest. My breathing grew shallow. I had no idea where I was shot, but I knew it was bad. Real bad.

Mother Superior crouched at my side, her wrinkly face bearing down on me. Her stale, old-lady, smell thick in the air. "Where did they go?" she demanded. "Where!"

"H-h-h-ome." The second the word left my mouth, my body went numb. My vision tunneled until I couldn't see anymore.

Chapter Two

~ Infiniti ~

I honestly had no idea how long I'd been holding my pee, but sitting there on the toilet with my bony butt cheeks on a thin layer of toilet paper I had meticulously laid out, you'd think I'd been holding it for days. Maybe even months. Heck, my stream flowed so loudly I could barely hear Dominique calling out that she needed to get something from the car.

"No!" Mrs. Wells hollered from the stall next to mine, jarring me back to the reality that we were still in danger and Dominique had just split!

I finished my business as fast as I could and raced out of the bathroom. When I burst out into the main section of the truck stop, I caught a glimpse of Mrs. Wells and Fleet as they tore through the glass doors and high-tailed it into the parking lot, shouting for Dominique. I started after them, when a security guard blocked the door. That's when I noticed all eyes in the store were on me.

"Umm, hello?" I said with a nervous laugh, wondering why I was suddenly so interesting to a store full of truckers in the middle of Nowhere, Michigan. Was it my hair? Did I have something on my face? I even glanced at my boots, checking for a trail of stuck-on toilet paper. Nothing.

The guard, who had a round baby-face and thick gut, pointed at the over-sized television hanging above the check-out counter. "Are they talking about you?"

HOLY CRAP! It was my mom, being interviewed by a reporter. Her eyes were bloodshot and encased in dark circles. Her hair frizzed into a complete nightmare of a mess. She held up a sign with a blown up picture of me eating waffles at our kitchen table. Of course she had to pick the most hideous photo of me she could find, complete with bedhead and maple syrup dripping from my chin. I mean, did she really think that was an okay picture?

"Coming on the heels of a gruesome car crash that killed Harmony High School student Dominique Wells and her family, the school is now faced with the horrible reality that two students are missing." The perfectly groomed reporter held the microphone to my mom's face. "Mrs. Clausman, how long has your daughter Infiniti been missing?"

"A week now, which is not like her." My mom's voice sounded hoarse, her nose clogged and stuffy. "I've tried her cell phone and my calls go directly to voice mail. She always calls me back. Always." My mom stifled a sob. "I can only assume she's been abducted because she's never been gone like this. Ever."

My body tingled with guilt. What had I done to her? Mom was normally feisty, over-opinionated, and crass— my being missing was sucking the life right out of her.

"Anything else you can share with us, Mrs. Clausman?"

"Yeah, to the assholes who took her, we're gonna find

you and throw your asses in jail! You hear me! You're gonna fry for this!"

Oh, there she is, I thought to myself with a slight chuckle, proud of my mom's renewed spunk.

The reporter lowered the mic, wide-eyed, and whispered something about watching her language before continuing. "Mrs. Clausman, anything else?

"Sorry," my mom said, clearing her throat. "Her friend from school Trent Avila is also missing."

The camera panned to Trent's little, old grandmother. She held a framed picture of him. Of course he looked tanned and gorgeous, all suited up in his school soccer uniform. I also saw a ton of people behind them, holding posters and candles.

Great.

"Mrs. Avila," the reporter said, leaning in and lowering her voice a little, the graveness of the situation causing her to pause for a second, "is there anything you'd like to say about your grandson?"

Trent's hunched grandmother held her cross in her hands. Tears flooded her cloudy, blue eyes. "He's gone. *Dios mio.* My boy. He's gone."

Did she say gone? As in dead? I shivered, wondering if she knew that Trent had been shot and killed in another time. Especially since Trent did say she could sense things.

My mom hugged Trent's grandmother and tears streamed down their faces. The image then switched to the reporter who flashed a phone number where people could call in "tips to the whereabouts of the missing Texas teens."

My blood chilled. My nerves skyrocketed. I felt like I had just been busted in a crime spree, even though I hadn't done anything but try to help my friend Dominique. I had no idea my mom would freak like that.

"Is that you?" the guard asked again, coming closer to me. "Are you in trouble?"

An uneasy laugh escaped my lips. "Well, uh, yes, that's me, but I'm not exactly—"

Fleet burst into the store. "Tiny, let's go!" he ordered.

The guard stepped back, pulled out his gun, and aimed at Fleet. The click-clack of a rifle filled the air, and I turned to see the cashier with his own firearm.

I threw my hands in the air, even though they weren't even pointing their weapons at me, and yelled, "I'm innocent!"

Talk about a dumb thing to say, but I had to say something!

"Hands on your head! Down on the ground!" the guard barked to Fleet.

Fleet's green eyes, which were once black as night, stormed over. His jaw clenched. "You don't want to do that."

"Don't hurt them," I said to Fleet, thinking that the weapon holders probably thought I was talking to them.

"I don't have time for this," Fleet said through gritted teeth. He flexed his hands at his sides and a gray mist collected at his fingertips. The lights overhead started to buzz and flicker.

"What in the hell?" the chubby guard said, his voice coated in disbelief.

Fleet flung out his hands. The guard fired his weapon. A whooshing stream of gray from Fleet pulsed through the store like a crazy light show at a concert, complete with laser beams and misty smoke.

I dropped to my knees and covered my head, waiting for a barrage of shooting and hollering. Nothing happened. Nada. Even the television had gone silent.

"Get up," Fleet said, standing over me.

I peered up at his angry face and then scanned the area. Everyone was frozen in place like wax figures. Even the news had paused.

Fleet held out his hand and helped me up. "Whoa," I said. "You can freeze stuff?"

Mrs. Wells charged in from the parking lot, but came to an abrupt stop when she noticed how time stood still. She approached the guard, plucked the hovering bullet out from mid-air, and then looked over her shoulder at the trucks and truckers outside. They too had stopped moving. She tossed Fleet a look.

Fleet rubbed the back of his neck. "It was necessary."

She palmed the bullet in her hand before dropping it in her pocket. "Dominique is gone."

"What?" Fleet asked.

"I lost her signature. Seems she's with someone who has the ability to cloak her."

Fleet paced around like an angry animal. He kicked the newspaper stand, sending papers all over the place. "Did you at least see what direction they were headed?"

"South. In a yellow rig. Shouldn't be too hard to find."

"Okay, then we head south."

Mrs. Wells came up to Fleet with a "you're not gonna like this" look on her face, an expression I'd seen on my mom many times. "I think we should split up. You take the Void home, and then track Dominique. I'll search for Colleen."

"Colleen?" Fleet asked. "She turned on us!"

"She's been my friend for lifetimes and I have to believe that I can reach her somehow. Or at least find out what she knows. There has to be a way to stop this madness." She rubbed her eyes. "She may be the key to saving my daughter."

Fleet gave her a puzzled look. "Caris, she'll kill you."

"Maybe. But I have to try."

Following their conversation like a tennis match, my head began to spin. "Hey," I cut in, and pointed to the television. "The entire freaking country is looking for me right now. It's all over the news."

"The news?" Mrs. Wells muttered to herself, no doubt considering the complication of a nationwide manhunt added to our messed-up situation.

"Yeah," I said, tearing up as I thought of my poor mom. "They're looking for me and Trent, the missing Texas Teens."

"Then you can't go home," Mrs. Wells said. "It'll be too dangerous for you and your family." Her determined stare softened. "I'm sorry, Infiniti. You'll have to stay with Fleet."

"But, I, uh…" My voice trailed off, the idea of being alone with Fleet terrifying me more than the prospect of danger back home in Houston.

"Fine, Tiny's with me," Fleet said. "But, Caris, you can't do this."

Mrs. Wells came up and held my arms, ignoring Fleet. "Fleet will take care of you, I promise. Right, Fleet?"

He gave a long pause before saying, "Yeah."

Mrs. Wells left me and placed her hand on Fleet's shoulder. "And, Fleet, I'm sorry for—" Her voice cracked and her lip quivered. "Everything." She reached into her coat pocket, I thought for the bullet she had put there, but instead pulled out Professor Huxley's journal. She handed it to Fleet.

"Keep it safe," she instructed. "There may still be a purpose for this book."

Mrs. Wells wound her way around the frozen security

guard and was almost through the double glass doors when I found my voice. "Wait!" She stopped and looked back at me, regret and defeat etched on her face. "How will we know if you find Colleen?"

Her long pause told me we'd never see her again. "Fleet will know."

I watched her walk away into the night until she disappeared from view, leaving me alone with Fleet, my own personal, fully equipped with anger-issues, bodyguard. Talk about a nightmare.

"Let's go," he ordered, shoving the leather journal in his jacket pocket.

We started to leave the truck stop when I spotted the chip aisle. My stomach growled and my mouth watered. "Hold up," I said.

I dashed around the counter, careful not to touch the motionless cashier, grabbed two plastic bags, and started stuffing them with Hot Cheetos. Then I darted to the soda cases and crammed in as many root beers as I could without busting the plastic wide open.

"Come on!" Fleet yelled.

Sprinting back to the front of the store, I stopped in my tracks, right in front of the alcohol section. Eyeing the wine labels but having no idea what was good or what was bad, I grabbed two bottles with the cutest names I could find: Precious Girl and Boo Boy. With a bottle under each arm, I made my way to my moody companion.

His glower could've killed me right then and there, but I didn't care. Trent was dead in the thirties, shot by a crazy ass nun who looked just like my old friend and his ex, and probably *was* her in some sort of weird past lives way. Dominique had split and joined up with some Transhuman who was hiding her from us. Mrs. Wells had gone off to find Colleen, and the whole freaking country was looking for me.

My thoughts turned to my mom—crying, desperate, and frantically searching for me. Guilt and remorse took me over and I started to shake. Tears filled my eyes and tiny sobs escaped my lips as we climbed in the car and took off in search of Dominique.

Fleet had been hauling down the highway, but eased up a bit when he clued in on the complete meltdown I was having. "Hey," he said. "You, ya know, okay?"

"Shut up," I blurted, wiping my face and turning away from. "I'm fine."

But I was nowhere near fine. And I had no idea how much more I could take.

Chapter Three

~ Dominique ~

My heart thumped against my chest like a jackhammer. My hands shook with fear. I tucked them under my legs so my Santa Claus look-alike driver couldn't see them. He might think I was some sort of strung-out runaway and that he should take me to the cops. Little did he know I had no home. In fact, I had nothing.

My friend Trent had been shot and killed in the 1930s while trying to protect me. My dad had been murdered by the Tainted. My love for lifetimes, Farrell, had turned on me and now hunted me. And I had just left the protection of my mom, my best friend, Infiniti, and Farrell's brother, Fleet in an attempt to keep them from harm. If Farrell wanted to kill me, he didn't have to kill everyone I cared about.

"Little lady, you're freezing." My driver reached over and cranked the heater. The stench of oil and leather filled the cabin of the big rig, clogging my throat. "I may have a blanket behind your seat if you want to look."

Muttering a thanks and stifling a cough, I shifted so I could feel around the floorboard behind me. Nothing. I stayed in that position and pretended to keep looking so I could peek out the back window, but couldn't see a thing. Facing forward again, I leaned down a bit and eyed the side-view mirror. The road behind us looked dark and empty.

Did I get away from Mom and Fleet that easily?

The eighteen-wheeler lurched, and that's when I noticed our speed. We were hauling. My stomach dropped. *Is this guy a murderer? Whisking me away to his "death cabin" somewhere?* My mind filled with all the horror movies I'd ever watched. Goosebumps lined my skin.

I eyed the speedometer—one hundred miles per hour! "Um, mister—"

"We gotta get away from the bad guys, right?" he said with a wink.

I shuddered, grossed out by his wink, when his phrase "bad guys" made me pause. When I had hopped in his truck, I had made up a story about being afraid of my drunk boyfriend. I never said anything about bad guys. I scooted away from him and closer to the door. My hand connected with the door handle, and a shock stung my fingers.

The man chuckled, but I detected a hint of nervousness in his laugh. "The cold weather always makes me shock myself," he said, rubbing his thick fingertips together.

Trying to act calm and not let on how freaked I was, I laughed back. "Um, yeah. The cold weather." I eyed the expansive road ahead of us. The only break in the darkness was the white stripes streaking past down the middle of the asphalt. If I flung open the door and jumped out of a speeding big rig going a hundred, I'd probably die. If I stayed, I might get killed. And then I remembered Farrell would eventually find me and end me anyway. So why should I care how I died? It was a stupid thing to think about, picking a preferred means of death, but for some reason, I felt the need to get away from crazy grandpa.

The lock at the top of the door was upright. That was good. I slipped my fingers around the door handle and scooted closer to my exit, deciding to take my chances with a stunt-move leap from the truck.

"Hey! What are you doing?" the old man called out, catching on to my plan.

"Getting away from *you!*" I pulled the handle and pushed, but nothing happened. It was locked after all! I clawed at the top of the door and pulled at the metal lever, but it wouldn't budge!

"Not so fast, Dom," my driver, now abductor, warned.

My eyes scanned the area around the console, looking for something I could use to protect myself, when his words sank in. *Did he just call me Dom?* My mind raced, trying to remember if I told him my name, but I knew I hadn't. Especially not *that* name. And then, a whispering recognition of someone calling me Dom entered my awareness, a memory lodged so deep in my brain it barely escaped.

I pressed up against the door, the cool glass tingling the back of my head. "Who the hell are you?"

"Shit," he muttered. A charge filled the air. His skin started glowing. His chubby Saint Nicholas body blurred in and out of focus as it morphed into a different shape. His middle shrank, his torso elongated, until he transformed into a tall, skinny guy my age with thick, brown hair and a narrow face. "Hey," he said. "Recognize me now? Dom, I'm—"

An explosion of wind gusted against the truck. I braced myself while the rig swerved to the right, tilted upward on its tires, and then thudded back to where it belonged. A crackling streak of light filled the night sky. Every hair on my body stood on edge.

"Farrell," I muttered, terrified.

"Son of a bitch!" The guy slammed his hands against the steering wheel and pulled back and forth. "Dom, listen to me. We don't have a lot of—"

Another electrified blast erupted, right in front of the truck. It pierced the asphalt and stayed lodged in its place for a second as if Zeus himself had flung the bolt directly from above. The truck swerved hard right to miss the spot. I was certain we were going to flip, but my companion compensated with a sharp turn in the opposite direction. The brakes screeched, the rig moaned, and if not for my seat belt, I would've hurtled through the windshield.

We came to an abrupt stop, the truck idling on the highway while we caught our bearings. My heart had lodged up in my throat. My skin prickled with fear. I searched the area for Farrell.

"Dom, listen," the guy whispered as he, too, scanned the roadway. "I'm here to help you."

Farrell came into view. Walking toward us with determined purpose, his body aglow, his arms swinging with lethal confidence. Talk about the perfect entrance for a blockbuster movie. Even the headlights shone on him as if he were the gorgeous star, making a grand entrance. Except he wasn't the hero anymore, he was the deadly villain.

"Open the glove box, pull out the metal collar inside, and fasten it around your neck." My driver pulled down his white t-shirt and showed me a snug, thick necklace. "It looks like this. Now hurry."

I eyed him like he was nuts, but right now, it was

either believe him and do as he asked, or let Farrell attack us. My fingers fumbled at the glove box. It fell open, exposing a dull, silver, neck collar. I picked it up and noticed the ends weren't connected.

"Put it around your neck and it'll close automatically."

The warm material hummed in my hands. I brought it up to my throat, but dropped my hands again before it touched my skin. I faced the guy who claimed he wanted to help me.

"Tell me who you are right the hell now." I eyed the approaching Farrell, placed the object on my lap and crossed my arms. "Or we're both dead."

The guy looked like he wanted to throttle me. "Still a smart ass, I see. Even at the most inopportune times." He exhaled, exasperated, the word *still* repeating in my head.

"What do you mean *still* a smart ass?"

He fidgeted, glanced at the ever closer Farrell, and faced me full on. "Dom, it's me, Jake. Your best friend from—"

A crashing crunch reverberated from the hood of the truck. Farrell! He had leaped onto the car, staring us down with emotionless eyes. I nearly jumped out of my skin, ready to slam the collar around my throat and take my chances with this Jake guy, when the object spilled out of my trembling hands and thudded onto the floorboard by my feet.

Farrell crouched down and glared at me through the windshield. "You can't run, Marked One."

Oh shit, I definitely wasn't his love of lifetimes any more. Instead, I was his target, destined for death.

"Get the collar!" Jake yelled.

Leaning down, I frantically patted around with my hands, looking for the metal band that had suddenly turned into my only hope.

Glass shattered. The windshield erupted in crystal showers. A blast of frigid air swept through the cabin. Electrified blasts sizzled all around me. I had no idea if Jake, or whoever he was, had the power to hold off Farrell, but I prayed he could. I stretched out my arms as far as I could until I felt something solid at my fingertips.

"Hurry!" Jake grunted.

Flicking the collar closer to me, I swooped it up and sat upright in my seat. Farrell had leaned into the cabin, his hands clamped around Jake's throat. Jake pressed his palms against Farrell's chest, trying to keep distance between them. They were both electrified with their auras. Farrell's was white, while Jake's was a pale yellow. Their vibrant hues sizzled and popped against each other.

"On," Jake managed to squeak out. "Now."

I brought the collar up to my chin. Farrell's hate-filled gaze followed my movement. "Wearing that won't change your fate," he warned.

"Do it!" Jake hollered.

I slammed the metal around my neck. It clicked together and tightened until pointy shards from the inside burrowed into my skin. A yelp escaped my lips.

"No!" Farrell yelled, reaching out for me. I couldn't tell if he wanted to help me or kill me. Jake flung a blast of power at him and then slammed his hand on my wrist. His yellow-hued mist coiled around my arm. My head spun. The seat beneath me slipped away, and my body tumbled into weightlessness.

A moment later, I found myself falling out of the sky and racing toward a body of water. I didn't have time to yell or plug my nose or even brace myself before I plunged into the choppy waves.

When I surfaced, I spotted Jake next to me, breaking

through the ripples and gulping for air. He slapped the water with his hands and started hollering with excitement. "We did it, Dom! We really did it!"

I combed my wet locks out of my face and spit out a mouthful of saltwater, searching the area. A sandy shoreline lay not too far in the distance. It was practically deserted — only a couple of beach houses dotted the landscape.

"Where are we?" I asked out loud.

He followed my line of sight. "I have no idea. I was actually thinking about a safe house I know of in Colorado." He shielded his eyes from the sun. "This is definitely not Colorado." He eyed me suspiciously, both of us wading in the water. "Wait a minute, what were *you* thinking of?"

My mind raced with the scene we had just escaped, the shocking realization that Farrell was going to kill me just like he killed my dad twisted tight in my gut.

A hand rested on my arm. "Hey," Jake said. "You okay?"

Anger quickly replaced my fear. "Okay? Am I... okay? Are you really asking me that? Do you even know me?" I started swimming away from Jake and to the shore, the sound of his stroke and kick trailing mine while I focused on what I was thinking of in that truck right before we disappeared.

I climbed out of the ocean and flopped down on the sand. Jake approached with caution wearing a black backpack that I hadn't noticed before. Sopping wet and looking timid, he knelt beside me, but not too close. "Man, they really did a number on you. You don't remember a damn thing, do you?"

"Galveston," I muttered. "I was thinking of Galveston Island right before we disappeared."

"Really?"

"Yeah, really." I ran my hand across the packed, brown sand and breathed in the salty air. "This must be it."

He studied the area. "Why Galveston?"

His gaze drifted from the sky to the waves, and then back to me, and I did a double take. "Your eyes, the color, they're brown?"

I sprang to my feet, suddenly suspicious of my so-called best friend Jake. "Pures have green eyes, not brown." Reaching for the collar around my neck, I pulled, expecting it to unhook, but it didn't. Instead, it got tighter with each tug, digging into my skin like a thousand tiny razors.

"Hey, relax!" Jake jumped up and held my shoulders. He breathed in and out, expecting me to copy him, but who the hell was he?

I struggled to dig my fingers in between my skin and the metal, but there was no room. Pressure started to close my windpipe. Blood dripped down my neck. My desperate lungs grappled for air.

Jake pried my hands away from the death object and pressed them against his chest. He lowered his voice, forcing me to quiet my gasping so I could hear him. "You've always loved the color blue. At first, when you were little, you liked a deep, dark blue. As you got older you started favoring the aquas." My breathing grew easier. "You've always been the kind of girl who doesn't like a ton of attention, the good, quiet girl who knows what she wants and doesn't put on airs to fit in or be like anyone else." My pulse slowed. "You've always been close to your parents, especially your dad. One of your favorite things to do with him is look for stones and fossils." A lone tear trailed down my cheek as I thought of Dad, dead because of me. "When you're afraid, or worried, you twist your hair. Once, to help you kick your habit, I taped your fingers together, but it still didn't stop you."

The collar loosened until it fit like a snug necklace, not like a death -grip device. The warm sun overhead disappeared behind thick clouds and my body shook with cold. Jake brought me in and hugged me tight. "I'm sorry," he soothed. "I hoped seeing me would somehow trigger your memories, but I guess it didn't."

"No, it didn't." I forced myself to pull it together and stepped away from him because I didn't know if I could stand to trust one more person who might betray me.

"We've got a lot to talk about, but first let me explain the collars." He fingers traced his. "I call them veils. They're used to cloak the energy field around us, rendering us invisible to any Transhuman, Pure or Tainted."

"Like the shield my mom and dad used to hide me?"

"Yes! Like that!" He tapped on his with his fingertip. "Except it's not controlled by anyone else. Neat, huh?"

"So no one can track me," I muttered. "Not even Farrell."

"Yep, not even him."

So much excitement covered his face you would've thought he was explaining to me that we had won the lottery.

"And the color of your eyes?"

He kicked at the sand. "I've been in limbo, trying to find you for lifetimes after being separated from the group. I think hanging out alone and with regular humans has dampened my power and altered my eye color. Or maybe it's the collar I'm wearing. I really don't know. But I swear I'm your best friend and I'm on your side."

"Oh," I said, not really sure how to respond to that.

"Now, one more thing and then we can catch up."

He reached into his jeans pocket and pulled out a rolled up piece of paper. "Shoot," he muttered. "I didn't count on a plunge in the ocean." He handed over the soggy object. "Hopefully you can still read it."

I gave the note a series of shakes, and then started unrolling. The paper felt thick and weathered and had been rolled so tightly the inside wasn't too saturated. Fully opened, I recognized my own handwriting right away. My bones chilled at the message.

Kill Farrell.

Chapter Four

~ *Trent* ~

My head spun. My body burned. My mouth felt like the desert. I didn't know where I was or what was happening when strong arms lifted me up and set me down on a hard surface. My chest and back exploded with pain. A loud yell wanted to shoot out of my mouth, but only a low moan escaped.

"Be careful with him," someone said.

"Yes, sir," a younger voice replied.

"Keep him awake," the first voice ordered.

The potent stench of sulfur wafted into my nasal passages, traveling all the way into my brain, and shook me. My eyelids cracked open to see a hand waving a small, white piece of cloth beneath my nose.

"Sir, his eyes are opening."

"Good. Now let's get him out of the church. Follow my lead."

The hand in front of my face disappeared from view, and my body felt like it was floating. A tall, domed ceiling with columns on either side whisked past. Lifting my head a tad, I saw a guy in a navy suit at my feet, back facing me, his hands grasping the handles of a stretcher. Another guy loomed over my head. He wore the same clothes. From my vantage point, I could see gold buttons lining his jacket. Not much older than me, he looked down at me with a worried face. I spotted a white, round emblem with a red cross on his hat.

"Which hospital are you taking him to?" I couldn't see her, but I recognized the commanding voice of Mother Superior. "Which one, boy?" she pressed.

I tried to get out the word "No," but couldn't.

"Jefferson Davis," one of the voices answered. "Now please, step aside."

We burst out of St. Joseph's church and into a crowd of people. The cold air felt good against my blazing forehead and cheeks. I tried to make out the faces around me, but everything kept fading in and out of focus.

"Make way," my carriers warned. "Step away for the injured."

The throng cleared. A boxy, black car came into view. I let my head fall back, the pain so intense my vision started to darken. My handlers lifted the stretcher, tilting it back and forth until they slid me all the way into the cab and shut the door.

"Drive fast, Matthew."

"Yes, Dad."

Hands prodded at my chest, ripping away my shirt, and then pressed hard. This time my voice found its yell and blasted it out like a canon. After it ended in a whimper, I went limp, exhausted at the involuntary exertion.

"Kid," a voice said up close by my face. "Stay with me, okay?"

"Dad, is he dying?" It was the younger voice, the driver. Matthew was it?

"Not on my watch," the dad declared.

Their conversation continued, but a fog invaded my brain and I couldn't hold on to any of their words. A hint of sulfur floated in the air. This time, it barely penetrated my sense and instead lingered around my head like a halo. I didn't care. Dominique and the others had made it back home. That was all that mattered. There was nothing for me in 1930.

"*There is something*," a low voice whispered. "*I promise*."

A fresh blast of sulfur exploded around me. It traveled up through my nose like a freight train, snapping me to consciousness. "Got you," the man said.

"Is he okay?" the young voice from the front asked. Was he driving?

A cool, wet cloth draped over my forehead. "For now."

The darkness in the car kept my rescuer shrouded in mystery. All I could see of him were his shiny, gold buttons. Round, over-sized, and perfectly polished. While I struggled to keep my focus on them, a glowing light behind the man came into view. Soft and shimmery, it floated around him, hovering as if trying to get closer to me but unable to do so in the cramped space.

An angel? A spirit orb?

I wanted to tell the man about the illumination, ask him if he could see it, but I couldn't. The effort to verbalize was no match for the struggle raging inside my damaged body. My body temperature shifted from blazing hot to ice cold. Goose bumps popped up all over my skin. Involuntary jerking overtook my limbs, the pain in my chest deepened, and I lost my sight.

"Faster, Matthew."

The car lunged forward. I could sense the man beside me frantically working on my chest, but I knew his efforts were futile. I felt nothing. I was as good as dead.

"Trent, take my hand. Please."

The pleading words came through to me, clear and urgent. My consciousness worked to wrap around their meaning, but my body was shutting down, and the request slipped away from my mind.

"Please, please, please. Come with me," the whispering voice cried. *"Before it's too late."*

My pain started to ease. My muscles slacked. My body drifted into that calm state just before slumber. Sleep—how I longed to be swept away into a dreamlike place.

"PLEASE!" The voice shrilled at my ear.

The wail forced my eyelids open. Fluorescent lights lit up the space like a bright sun. I blinked, trying to adjust my vision. People in white gowns and hospital masks bustled all about me.

"Doctor, he's awake!" a female voiced exclaimed.

People all around me broke out into frantic action. A mask slammed down, covering my nose and mouth. A hazy glow from above drifted down, like a balloon losing its air. It held my attention, and I watched as it glided beside me. The glimmering mist stretched out and took on the shape of a girl. Young, big green eyes, dressed in white. An angel?

"I'm not an angel, but I am here to help you." She took my hand. A pulling sensation gathered at my fingers. She laughed. "You don't even know what you can do."

"I kind of know," I answered, thinking of being a Transhuman Supreme, but not knowing exactly what that meant. And then I realized I was standing beside the girl, her hand in mine.

"See?" Her wide eyes held mine. "You can do a lot."

She pointed. My body lay flat on an operating table.

Doctors and nurses surrounded me. I didn't want to see them cut into my chest, so I turned to face the girl. "Am I dead? Am I a ghost?"

"You are in the space between." She squeezed my hand. "And I'm going to stay with you until you're better."

Better... I closed my eyes. The pain ravaging my chest had disappeared. The exhaustion inside me had vanished. I eyed the girl. "Who are you?"

"I'm Abigail. I'm your grandfather's friend. I'm going to help you get back to Dominique."

"Dominique? You know her?"

She smiled. "Yes, I know her. And she needs you now more than ever."

Chapter Five

~ Infiniti ~

I hated crying. Hated sympathy. And I especially hated having mascara running down my face. I wiped at my cheeks, and then realized I didn't even have any makeup on in the first place. I bet I looked like dog crap.

"Hey," Fleet said. "Infiniti. Are you okay?"

As if calling me by my name would make me feel better. Guys were such dumb asses. I gave a sigh to signal my annoyance. "Just hurry."

I couldn't think about my poor mom or Trent's grieving grandmother. We needed to find Dominique because finding her was the only way out of this mess. Or so I told myself because I didn't know what to think or what to do. Rescuing Dominique had turned into my only glimmer of hope.

"Okay," Fleet muttered, speeding back up again. "I'll hurry."

The dark highway stretched out for miles without sign of any other vehicles. As we drove, my mind raced with the idea of being stuck with Fleet for the rest of my life. I shuddered at the pure horror of it all, angry that fate couldn't have at least stuck me with a normal dude. Although it wouldn't hurt if he was as hot as Fleet.

"There she is." Fleet growled, flooring it and sending the jeep screaming forward.

My body tensed. I straightened in my seat, peering at the lone truck in the distance. As we zoomed closer, I noticed it was stationary on the side of the road. Maybe even broken down. "How can you tell that's her?"

An explosion of lightning erupted around the truck, streaking up into the sky like a beacon. My slight frame jerked with the blast, and a scream shot out of me.

"Oh, that's h-h-how," I stuttered, barely able to find my voice as fear hammered away at my chest.

I gripped my knees, sure we were going to barrel into the eighteen-wheeler, when Fleet threw his arm across my chest and slammed on his breaks. My torso pressed against the seat, the sheer force of Fleet's manpower pinning me back like a rag doll. The car screeched to a halt a mere inches away from the rig.

"Stay here," Fleet ordered. He hopped out of the car and made his way to the front of the truck. I did as he commanded... for about five seconds. No way in hell was he leaving me defenseless in an old, beat up Jeep. Besides, I was a Void and immune to all their energy flinging skills. I knew I'd be okay.

Tiptoeing, I followed Fleet's path, my breathing silenced, my nerves whacked out, images of Dominique's dead body filling my head.

"Please, powers of the natural world, let her be okay," I said to myself.

I crouched down near the hood of the truck and peeped around the bulky bumper. Fleet and Farrell stood an arm's length apart, shoulders square, their hands fisted at their sides. Two hot and sexy brothers who wanted to kill each other. This would be so good if it were a movie.

Instead, it was terrifying, and I wondered who would win if they faced off.

"Where the hell is she?" Fleet demanded.

"I should be asking *you* that question," Farrell replied, his tone icy and cold.

What? Dominique's gone? My stomach dropped. I quickly analyzed my choices. Jump out and demand to know what they meant about Dominique being gone or stay back and listen.

"You know, forget it. What I want to know is why you did it," Fleet said accusingly. "Was I nothing to you? Did being your brother mean *nothing*?"

Did what? I held back, intent on getting answers because I knew Fleet would never tell me anything.

Farrell took two steps back. "It wasn't like that."

"The hell it wasn't."

"We thought you had turned."

Fleet laughed, combing his hands through his hair. "Bullshit."

Cars started to zoom past, the temperature plunged to freezing, and the night air chilled me until I shook. I tucked my icy hands under my armpits.

"You violated your directive," Fleet accused.

Farrell took another step back. "None of it matters now that I have to end her."

Sparks flickered around Fleet's hands. "It matters to me, and I'm not going to let you."

Shit! They were about to go at it! If something happened to Fleet, I would be next. I burst into view. "Stop!"

Fleet glanced at me over his shoulder, firing his usual pissed-off glare in my direction. "Get the hell back, Tiny."

A pack of cars hurtled by. One honked, as if warning

us to be careful. Taking their advice and ignoring Fleet, I moved into the space between the brothers and smack dab in front of the headlights.

My teeth chattered as I studied Farrell, wondering if being friends with him, even for a little while, would help him take pity on me. "If-f-f Dominique is gone, then g-g-o. Leave us alone."

Vapor poured out of Farrell's hands and wrapped around his wrist. "I can't do that, Infiniti. I'm sorry."

Fleet pushed me out of the way. My body slammed against the hood of the truck before falling down on the street. Sparks exploded over me like the Fourth of July. Smoky plumes danced across my line of sight, and I could barely make out Farrell and Fleet. I swished the energized particles away with a rapid wave. Clearing the air, I saw Farrell and Fleet with their hands wrapped around each other's throats. Their bodies lit up as if flares emitted from within them.

"Don't make me do this," Fleet gritted out.

Their bodies lifted off the ground. Their auras sizzled against one another.

"I have no choice," Farrell said, his words empty of emotion, but his face giving away his conflict. "I'm sorry, brother."

A thousand ideas collided in my head, but one overrode the others — *get the hell out of the there.*

I sprinted back to the Jeep. Cars were halted on both sides of the highway, looking on as Farrell and Fleet exploded with light and rage.

"Young lady," a man said, sticking his head out his window. "Are you okay?"

I ignored the voice and jumped into the safety of my car. Farrell was about to obliterate Fleet. And even though I didn't completely trust my newly appointed bodyguard, he was all I had. Plus, I knew that deep down he cared for Dominique, and even me. Farrell, on the other hand, had turned into something purely evil, an assassin set on killing Dominique and anyone else who got in his way.

I leaned my forehead against the steering wheel and pressed my skin against the worn leather. "Now what?" I muttered out loud.

Blinking red lights reflected through the rear-view mirror. Sirens wailed in the distance. "Oh no, not the cops," I said to myself. I threw the car into gear and, knowing what I needed to do, I swerved around the big rig and stopped. I hopped out and yelled, "We'll help you!"

Farrell eyed me. He was listening! "Look, Dominique is gone, and we both want to find her, right? So let's team up and look for her and fight it out later. Okay?"

Farrell and Fleet's generated power fired down, their bodies returning to their normal hue. They released each other, yet stayed close.

"I will track your efforts and communicate with you as needed," Farrell said. "Double cross me, and you're both dead." He pointed at Fleet. "We'll finish this later."

"Damn straight we'll finish this later," Fleet hissed under his breath.

Smoky tendrils oozed out of Farrell's hands and wrapped around his body until he faded from view. A small crowd approached, frantic murmurings filled the air, and the wailing of police sirens grew louder.

"Is that the missing girl from Texas?" someone asked in a hushed tone.

"From the news?" someone else added.

Phones came out, lighted screens illuminated the worried and awe stricken faces of the Michigan travelers.

"Oh!" I said with a laugh. "Yeah, that's me, but I'm not—"

Fleet latched on to my wrist and yanked, pulling me to the jeep. "Come on," he ordered.

"Okay!"

When we got in the car, the concerned onlookers turned into activists. They surrounded the Jeep and demanded my release. I was actually touched at their concern, until Fleet fired up the engine.

"If these newfound fans of yours take you, you'll be returned home where it's not safe. You get me, Tiny?"

I thought of Dominique's mother and her warning that if I returned home, my mom and I would be at risk, and that was the last thing I wanted. My poor mom had been through enough.

A police car pulled up two cars behind us. "Over here!" Someone called out to the approaching cops.

Fleet cursed under his breath. "This is great."

He shifted the car into gear, rolling forward so that the bodies blocking our path would get out of the way. I leaned over and laid on the horn, waving them aside with my hands.

"Move it!" I yelled.

The highway bystanders frantically darted out of the way. I couldn't help but smile at my handy work, ready for another horn blasting, when shots rang out. I ducked while Fleet floored it.

Tires screeched, bullets lodged into metal, and an army of sirens blared at the heels of our vehicle. I kicked my stash of Hot Cheetos, sodas, and wine to the side of the floorboard and crawled down into the tight space. I studied Fleet. His eyes were narrow and fixed straight ahead, his jaw clenched. I almost yelled at him to hurry, but stopped because his eyes looked odd. Flickering with flashes of light, they started glowing. Sparks and vapor flowed around him.

"Hold on, Tiny."

The car took off like a rocket. I hugged the car seat in front of me, holding on for dear life, our supersonic speed forcing my face to practically become one with the cushion. My cheeks tingled. My scalp prickled with fear. And then, we stopped.

"We're safe," Fleet said.

I lifted my head and perked up my ears. "We are?"

"For now."

The car door opened with a creak while Fleet got out. In slow motion, I lifted myself from my safe place and peered out the window, my hands shaking as if I were a strung-out junkie on detox. I blinked, adjusting to the thick darkness, when light from inside a nearby cabin flicked on.

Thank God, I thought to myself. *A hide out.* I pushed my wild hair out of my face and grabbed my stolen necessities. Clutching the plastic bags to my chest, I shuffled to the front door. Tall and naked trees surrounded the abode. A light dusting of snow sprinkled the ground. The closer I got to what I thought might be a cozy place to chill and get a bath, the more I realized the place was a dump. Immediately, I thought of the run-down home of Trent's ancestors in 1930s Houston. I stopped dead in my tracks and shuddered. Nothing good happened in the 1930s.

Nothing.

Freezing cold and one vapor breath away from an ugly cry, I trudged up to the house. I opened the door and eyed the newly lit fire. Usually a symbol of warmth and cheer, this fire reminded me of the people I had lost—my friend Veronica, my neighbor Jan, Trent, Dominique's dad, and maybe even Dominique herself.

"All dead," I whispered to myself.

"What?" Fleet asked, his boots thudding against the wood floor as he inspected the interior of the house.

"Nothing," I muttered, flopping down on the drab, floral-print couch, and spacing out. Staring at the tongues of fire, I thought for sure I wouldn't live this out. Knew, without a doubt, that my first life was coming to an end. I held the wine bottles up to Fleet, ready to escape my messed up reality.

"Let's get drunk."

Chapter Six

~ Dominique ~

I had written a note to myself to kill Farrell?

A cloud must've covered the sun, because everything went dim — the weathered message in my hand, the sand at my feet, and the hope that somehow Farrell wouldn't kill me and we'd eventually be together.

Jake took the paper and stuffed it back into his jeans pocket. "Hey, let's check out that house and get out of the cold."

A violent wind whipped around us as we crossed a rickety bridge that went over the dunes and ended in a small yard of weeds and ant piles. The house, painted a rich blue with orange trim, towered over a concrete slab on tall cement beams. It looked empty. White shutters covered the windows, and there were no signs of tire marks on the driveway. A wooden gate, secured with a rusted padlock, blocked our path up the stairs.

"Great," I chattered, the cold water from our ocean plunge penetrating deep into my bones. "Now what?"

"I got this," Jake said.

He cupped his hands, blew into them, and then rubbed them together. He touched the keyhole of the lock with his index fingers. With a zap, the lock came undone. He stepped aside and smiled. "After you."

Another door met us at the second floor. It opened with a hard pull and we found ourselves in a screened-in porch. Chair cushions and a white cooler were stacked in one corner. On the other end of the porch were wooden rocking chairs, the kind you see in front of a country store. Of course, there was one more door to get through before entering the house.

Jake worked his Transhuman skills on the last barrier between us and warmth. Once inside, we found ourselves in an open room with a kitchen on the right, living room with a TV on the left, and a study just beyond.

"Heat," I said, scanning the walls for a thermostat.

Jake nodded to the far end of the room. "I see it."

The low rumble of a furnace shook the house and a slight burning smell filled the room. I stood frozen in place for a minute, waiting for the warmth, and took in the cozy beach house. The place had pale green walls, light-colored wood floors, and a massive kitchen with a long granite counter. I could definitely hang here.

Jake put his hands on my shoulders. "Let's get out of these wet clothes."

I stepped back and crossed my arms. "Excuse me?"

"Not like that. I mean, let's search the rooms for some dry clothes." He laughed. "Besides, we tried dating once, and it didn't exactly work out."

"We did?"

"Yeah." He smiled. "You drove me crazy, so I had to end it."

He started searching the rooms and left me alone with my thoughts. All this time I had thought Farrell was the only one for me. But if I had a thing with Jake, then what other secrets dwelled in my past? I had seen a glimpse of one of my prior lives back at Richard and Sue's cabin, but because of everything that had happened, I never got to see more. Now, here I was with someone who could fill in the gaps. But did I really want to know about them? Did it even matter? This was the first time any of us had lived beyond my killing of Tavion back in that red desert, so why would my past lives matter? I was beginning to think there was no escaping my final death.

Jake handed me a pile of clothes. "According to a stack of mail in the master bedroom, this is the home of Joanne and Bert Jones. They live in Beaumont, Texas. Hopefully they're our size."

"Yeah, and hopefully they won't be coming to their beach house any time soon." I took the outfit he had picked out for me and ducked into the hall bath.

"Hey! The pantry and fridge are stocked!" Jake called out excitedly while I peeled off my wet boots and soaking clothes, bra and all. Wrapping myself in a towel, I thought of the Petoskey stone Trent had given back to me in 1930. It was one of the stones my dad and I had found at Elk Rapids Beach. I had given it to Trent on Christmas Eve. It was my only memento of him and of my dad and I had plopped it in my boot.

I eyed the wet heap of fabric on the floor. *Please let it be there*, I thought to myself, fearful that it had washed out of my boot during my Gulf Coast plunge. Tipping my boot over, it spilled out, along with a splash of saltwater. I held the stone tight, telling myself that having it was a good sign.

"You need anything?" Jake called out.

"No, I'm fine." With my body finally dry, I unfolded the stack of clothes Jake had handed me, relieved to find that he had included a bra and some underwear. Squeezing into gray sweat pants that were a tad too short and a blue hoodie with sleeves that barely reached my wrists, I secured the stone in my pants pocket. The ensemble wasn't a perfect fit, but I was happy with anything dry and comfy. When I exited the bathroom, Jake tossed me a pair of fuzzy socks. Wearing black sweats and no shirt, I spotted a long chain with a charm hanging from his neck. He pulled on a sweatshirt before I could take a closer look.

"You hungry?" he asked.

"Not really," I said, taking a seat on the white couch. I pulled up my legs and wrapped my arms around them. I thought of the people who had died because of me, especially Trent and my father, and I didn't know if I could ever forgive myself for that.

Jake moved his backpack off the couch and sat next to me. "I know what you're doing."

I studied the top of his metallic collar peeking out of his sweatshirt and forced myself to sense mine against my skin because the longer I had it on, the more it didn't feel like I was wearing it. It was as if it had turned into a second skin or something.

"You're over analyzing things, Dom."

So many deaths were on me. So many lives altered because of my doomed fate. And for what? So a teenage girl could live? Sure my parents and Farrell had said I was special and I was marked, but I still didn't completely understand it. It was something I really hadn't been able to wrap my head around.

"It drives me nuts when you get like this, you know," he said, poking my side.

And that's when I snapped, like a mental patient coming out of a haze. "What do you mean, 'you know?' As if I even know anything? How about you tell me what *you* know. Huh? Let's try that for a change!"

Jake sat back a little, the higher octave of my voice pushing him away from me. But then he moved in again, his eyes softening. "You don't know everything?" he whispered.

The anger inside me started to cool, doused by his concern. And then guilt set in for losing it like that, especially since he wasn't to blame for anything. "No, I don't. Over my lifetimes, I remember less and less until this life where I apparently remember nothing." I shook my head. "I mean, I've been filled in on some, but I've never been able to get a full picture of everything. It's like not being able to see every scene in a really long and terrifying movie. A movie I'm not so sure I want to watch. And it's driving me crazy."

He rubbed my knees, and suddenly, it felt as if he really was my best friend. As if I had needed him all this time. "Let's start with what you know. Okay?"

His request seemed reasonable enough. "Well, this is my ninth and final life. Tavion, the leader of the Tainted, has killed me in each one. Mom and Dad have always protected me." I paused, thinking of my dad, tears pricking at my eyes. "But now my dad is dead. Along with my friend Trent. And Farrell, my boyfriend all my lifetimes, who was originally assigned as my Walker, has to kill me. His brother, Fleet, who'd been infiltrating the Tainted, has returned and wants to help. But there's something about him I just can't figure out. He's cocky and irritating, and I don't know if I can trust him."

Jake's hands fell off my knees. His eyes took on a faraway look. "Whoa," he whispered.

"What?" I whispered. "What is it?" A howling wind

whistled through a black, freestanding fireplace in the corner. Every ounce of warmth in the room quickly evaporated, and a cold shiver crawled over my skin.

"I'll tell you what I know, Dom. I promise. But first, do you know about the prophecy?"

My thoughts transported me to the beach, the safe place where Farrell and I had said our good-byes before he told me to run. With the pain in my heart freshly renewed, I repeated Farrell's words. "First will be the changing that comes from within. Second will be the changing that comes from without. Third will be the demise of those linked to the One."

"That's right. Now what do you think it means?" Jake asked. "The changing from within," he repeated, as if trying to figure it out, but I already knew.

"When I defeated Tavion, his blood mixed with mine and I almost turned Tainted."

He whistled. "Really?"

"Yeah, really. He was a part of me." I clasped my hands together and shuddered, remembering my haunting by the creepy girl who was really a manifestation of the evil within me. Jake must've thought I was trying to warm myself because he draped a blue blanket over my lap.

"The changing from without," he said. "What could that mean?"

"Without," I repeated, as if saying the word out loud would force something to come to mind. And then I thought of ditching Mom, Fleet, and Infiniti at the truck stop. I flung the cover off my lap. "Oh, no."

I paced the room, desperate to remove the metal around my neck, but terrified of yanking at it. Instead, I twisted a strand of hair so tight around my finger my head hurt.

"Calm down," Jake said. He blocked my circular path. "Ease up, okay?" He untwisted the hair from my fingers and stared down at me. Man, his eyelashes were long. "Explain."

"I've never been without my friends, and now I am. Get it? Without. Something horrible is going to happen to me *without* them. And then everyone will be screwed." I pointed to my tight necklace. "Take it off."

"What?" Jake said. "No way. That thing is keeping you hidden and alive."

"Well, I don't care. They need to find me. I want it off. Right now."

He backpedaled to a chair and flopped down. "You have no idea what you're saying."

Suddenly, I felt like a prisoner, trapped against my will. Plus, who the hell was this Jake person anyway? "You take this off right now, or I'm outta here." I stomped over to the door and gripped the handle, waiting for him to say something.

"You're safer with it on."

"Safe! Are you kidding? I've been killed eight times now! And just to enlighten you, this life isn't going so hot either!" I pounded at the door, letting my frustration out. "Where the hell have you been anyway? My so-called-best friend!" The more I went on, the angrier I got, as if I had just been given a license to go bat-shit crazy. "I don't even know why all of this is on me! I didn't do anything to deserve this!"

I knew I had gone too far when I heard my blasting voice echoing through the vacation home. Forcing myself to pull it together, I noticed Jake's head hanging low. A low whisper came from him. I approached him slowly, hoping he'd repeat himself.

"I'm really sorry, Dom."

"Sorry?"

"I lied about being separated from the group." He rubbed his face. "I left you after first life. Abandoned ship. Decided to save my own skin and turn my back on the mission." He let out a sigh. "I was a coward, letting you and the others face Tavion alone. That's why I haven't been there for you."

Defeated, I slunk down beside him. "Why'd you come back?" I asked, my voice broken, hot tears stinging my eyes.

"Because you did it. You defeated Tavion. After all this time. So I got my ass in gear, gathered up these harnesses I had been working on, and set out to rescue you."

He turned to face me full on. "There's so much we need to talk about, and we'll have plenty of time, but you need to understand why this all started."

"This?"

"Why you're the marked one. Why Tavion branded you."

I searched my mind for everything I had been told about Tavion and my mark. "My parents said I was born with the mark in each life. Jan and Abigail explained that it was the doing of Tavion, that he had injected a piece of his essence into me so that when our blood mixed he could take me over. But no one ever mentioned why."

Jake raised an eyebrow. "Jan and Abigail?"

"Abigail is a Transhuman girl who sacrificed herself for me, and Jan is a lady that lived across the street from me in Houston. She's dead now."

"Oh," Jake said. He rubbed his knees and shifted, waiting for me to say something, but I couldn't. He knew my past lives and I didn't. "Hey, we can talk about this later if you want. We don't have to do it now."

"None of them ever said why," I muttered. "After everything I'd been through, you think they would've told me. Why." It wasn't a question, but a statement acknowledging how little I knew about my fate. My deaths. Everything.

My heart ached so bad I thought it was crushing inside of me, breaking into tiny pieces, the kind that could never be mended. The desire to know grew stronger with each empty beat. "Tell me."

The hum of the furnace silenced, as if it knew Jake had something monumental to say and wanted to listen in. "Dom, your dad"—he drew in a deep breath—"wasn't always a Pure. He was born and raised Tainted."

He let his revelation sink in, waiting for me to say something, but I had no words. "He switched sides when he fell in love with a Pure. Your mom. Tavion lost his mind when your dad left. He declared your dad a traitor. Made his life a miserable hell. It was beyond awful. And then, when the Tainted and Pure decided to let their war rest on the fate of one soul, Tavion chose you."

"To get back at my dad."

"Yes. The ultimate payback."

Everything came back to my dad. The weight of his death fell heavy on me, like a hundred thousand weights crushing down on my very soul. "So Tavion hated him because he switched sides?"

"Dom." He waited a few seconds. I could see an internal struggle in his eyes. As if he knew his words would hurt me. "Your dad and Tavion. They were..." He paused. "Brothers."

A blast of sickening surprise shot through my veins.

"Brothers?" The furnace kicked back on. The walls of the house shook. And even though a fresh wave of warm air entered the room, my body started chilling to the bone. "Tavion was my uncle?"

"Yeah." Jake sighed. "That's probably why your parents didn't tell you. To them, he wasn't family anymore. He was just the bad guy."

I shuddered. My head cluttered with fresh terror. The idea of Tavion wanting to kill me, his own flesh and blood, repulsed me. And even though I had killed him in the end, I was still in danger, his evil plan for my demise taking shape in Farrell.

"There's one more thing you need to know."

"Oh God," I muttered, tightening every muscle in my body and waiting for whatever blow he had left to level.

"You're right that Farrell is, or was, your Walker, assigned to protect you, but you're wrong that he's been your love for lifetimes."

My lip quivered. Farrell wasn't my true love? I didn't get it. And then I eyed Jake. He was tall and attractive with thick brown hair and amazingly long eyelashes, and he seemed like a decent guy. Were we in love? Is that what he had meant when he said we had a thing but that it didn't work out? Is that why I felt so comfortable around him?

"Were we...?"

"No, I mean, not that I didn't try or anything, but in our first life you were in love with someone else. Head over heels. You were even betrothed."

"Betrothed? As in almost married?"

"Yes."

"To who?"

"Fleet."

Chapter Seven

~ Trent ~

I was ready to die. Had given up on living. But this little girl had somehow pulled my soul out of my body to tell me that Dominique needed my help. Standing in an operating room surrounded by 1930's archaic technology and medicine, I didn't want to believe her, but how could I not? I was experiencing a miracle. Even though she said she wasn't an angel, I knew something divine was happening to me.

"Come on," she said.

She took my hand and led me straight through the double doors and almost directly into two police officers. Startled, I stumbled back.

"They can't see us," the girl said with a laugh.

My body tingled all over from passing through the thick wood, and a strange ringing filled my ears. *What's happening to me?* I turned my attention to the men in front of me. I waved my hands back and forth in front of their faces. They didn't budge. Long coats, tall hats, a weapon in one holster and a long baton in the other—their stiff demeanor reminded me of the royal guard.

I glanced back at the operating room, then eyed the cops again. "Why are they here?"

"You'll see," the girl said.

People crowded the dingy and dark hallway. Occupied hospital beds lined the walkway. The more I examined the nearby faces, the more I realized they were all minorities like me—Hispanic and African American. The only white people were the staffers.

"What kind of hospital is this?" I muttered.

Two figures in navy coats rushed down the long corridor, weaving in and out of people, wheelchairs, and gurneys. More cops? But then I spotted the white cross emblem on their hats. Gold buttons lined their jackets. Were they the father and son from the ambulance?

"How is he?" the father asked as he neared.

"Yeah, is he going to make it?" the son chimed in. I searched my memory for his name, but couldn't find it.

The cops looked straight ahead, ignoring them.

"That's my transport in there," the father said, concern and anger lacing his frustrated words. "I have a right to know, dammit."

The older cop cleared his throat and said reluctantly, "The doc says he'll pull through. He's to be transported to the jail once he's stabilized."

My stomach plunged. *Jail?*

"On what charge?" the son demanded.

The cop sneered and clenched his jaw. The dad leaned in. "You know as well as I do that it will be public record, Danny. So you may as well tell me."

Ah, so he knew the cop. Made sense that the hospital transport would know the local police. But what didn't make sense was why the officers wanted to take me to jail and why the father and son had taken such a keen interest in me.

"The suspect is to be booked on charges of the

murder of three teens, per the Mother Superior and her statement."

Panic clutched at me. Fear prickled at my scalp. *Murder?*

The father got up in the cop's face. His eyes stormed over. "You can't finger the kid for a crime if there ain't no victims, even if his skin *is* brown."

The cop's eyes narrowed at the duo. "If you know what's good for ya, you'll stay out of this, Roland."

Roland? I inched up to the ambulance drivers. Closer inspection revealed tan skin, dark hair and eyes. They were Hispanic, like me. They must've taken pity on the poor Mexican boy shot and all alone. It made me wonder about my great grandparents, and if they knew what had happened to me.

"We'll see about that, Danny," Roland said.

The dad and his son left. I wanted to follow them, but the young girl had other ideas. She tugged on my fingers. "This way."

"But that dad. He can help me."

"Don't worry. You'll see him again."

She pulled me along the corridor to the nurse's station. "After your surgery, they'll put you in there." She pointed at the empty room across from the busy area. "When you start feeling better, you'll have to sneak out and go this way." She led me toward a dark hall lined with boxes one either side. A small exit sign hung from the ceiling.

"You want me to escape?"

She looked over her shoulder at me and nodded. "Uh-huh."

A zapping shock shook my brain. My body twitched. The young girl sped up, pulling me into a jog. "Hurry, you're waking," she warned. We made it to the end of the hall and in front of a door. "This is the stairwell. You need to go all the way down to the first floor. Once there, you'll be able to get out using the side exit."

Tiny jolts flashed in my head. My vision blinked in and out of focus. My fingers trembled. "Assuming I make it outside, then what?"

She pulled me down to her level. "I'll help you. Don't worry." She kissed my forehead. "You are blessed."

The soft touch of her lips on my forehead faded until only pressure remained, as if someone had been poking my brain. Pain radiated throughout my body. I struggled to pry open my eyes.

"He's coming to," a man's voice said. He pulled a needle out of my arm and stepped away from me. "Please keep this short, officers. This young man is my responsibility while he is in my care, and I will take this up with the judge if your questioning harms him in any way."

Shuffling sounded around me. A bright light warmed my face. "Kid. Kid. Can you hear me?"

My eyes fluttered open and I lifted my hand. "Yeah, I hear you," I croaked out. My parched throat ached, my dry lips cracked. The cops from the hallway were leaning over me. A nurse brought a cup of water to my face and slipped a straw in my mouth. I drew in a drink, and tried to sit up.

The older cop, Danny, glared at me. "Kid, you're in a heap of trouble, but if you tell us where the teens are, the ones that were with you in the church, I'll make sure you get off easy."

What was I going to say? My muddled brain needed time to think because there was no way I could tell him the truth. He'd have me locked up in an insane asylum. "Shouldn't you issue me my Miranda warnings or something?"

Danny looked over his shoulder at his partner, then back at me. He pulled out a small notebook and a pen. "Miranda? Is that the name of one of the teens you murdered? I mean, one of the teens you were with?"

"I said Miranda warning. You know, my rights."

He scowled, shoving his pad back in his pocket. "Listen, punk, you ain't got no rights. See? The only thing you got is a murder charge waiting to be filed against you. Unless, you tell me where those teens are."

Great, obviously Miranda rights weren't established yet. So now what? Stall. I started coughing. A few hacks at first before I really went for it. I rolled my eyes back in my head. I jerked my body up and down and kicked my legs.

"Out!" the doctor ordered the cops. "Now."

The nurse shuffled the uniformed men out of the room. The doctor started checking my vitals. When the cops were out of view, I slowed my coughing and stilled my body.

The doctor shined a light in my eyes and grunted. "Nurse, tell the officers the patient cannot be bothered today."

"Yes, Doctor."

He perched himself on the edge of the bed, waiting for the nurse to exit the room. He studied me with an inquisitive eye. "That was quite a performance, young man."

"I'm innocent."

He folded his arms. "Whatever happened at St. Joseph's is not for me to judge. Your care is my top priority, not the accusations of an antiquated church and a prejudiced judicial system." I could tell he wanted to say more, but he stopped himself. "Son, do you have family we can contact?"

I thought of my great grandparents, but what could they do? And then I thought of Abigail. Her tiny voice telling me how to get out and that she'd help me. "No. I'm all alone."

"I see."

He got up and went for the door. "Wait, Doctor, how bad off am I?"

"The bullet entered your chest, two centimeters above your heart. We were able to remove it with no complications. You got real lucky. Other than being sore for a few weeks, you'll have a full recovery." He waited to see if I had any questions, but I had none. "In your present condition, the authorities will have to wait for further questioning. But I can only guarantee a few days, understand?"

"Yeah, I understand."

Finally alone, I surveyed my condition. Tightly wrapped chest. Itchy hospital gown. And an overwhelming need to sleep. My gaze roamed around the room. No clock. No phone or TV. Was television even invented in the thirties? I couldn't remember. My brain had started to shut down, my eyelids growing so heavy I could barely keep them open. And it didn't matter. Nothing mattered, but sleep.

"*And the plan,*" Abigail's tiny voice whispered.

"The plan," I muttered slowly.

"*To escape.*"

"To esc..."

***

My body jerked. My eyelids flew open. I had no idea where I was, until my terrifying reality fell on me. *Hospital.*

Cops. Murder. Escape. Tossing off my covers, I shuffled my achy body to the window and peered out into the darkness. How long had I been asleep? Hours? Days?

"You need to leave now."

My heart jolted with fright, and I spun around to see a figure in my room. A guy about my age dressed in an old-fashioned soldier's uniform. I pressed my back up against the white wall and studied him. The details of his face were out of focus. His body blurry. When another soldier walked straight through the wall and joined the other, a cold sweat broke out over my body.

"He's awake?" the second soldier asked.

"Yep," the first soldier said. "And he has no idea what's happening."

The second soldier moved closer to me. When he did, his features shifted in and out of focus, too. And that's when I knew they were ghosts.

"Listen, friend," he said, "you need to get your clothes out of that there wardrobe, change, and get out of here quick." He pointed at a dingy brown dresser in the corner that I hadn't noticed before.

"Before the officers guarding your door come back," the first soldier added. "You hear?"

They eyed me, their forms blurring at the edges, their faces hazy and vague. With a hard swallow, I said, "Y-y-yeah. I hear you."

Fear chilled my body while I slipped out of my hospital gown and into the jean overalls and shirt I had been wearing when I was shot in the church. A large bloodstain on the fabric marked the spot where I had been shot, reminding me of everything that had happened in the sanctuary.

"Come on now," one of the ghosts said.

"Dumb chap is taking too long," the other whispered back.

My chest had started burning and a line of sweat dripped down my back. "I've been shot!" I yelled, then realized I was arguing with ghosts. I wiped my forehead. "God, I'm losing it," I muttered to myself.

Two more fuzzy figures appeared in my room, ladies in long, drab dresses. "They're coming back!"

A shot of adrenaline propelled me to the door. I curled my fingers around the small brass knob, drew in a deep breath, and then eased it ajar. I peered about—all clear. As I stood there, more shadowy figures emerged from the rooms—women, men, some uniformed, some not, and some children. They rushed me like an angry mob, bombarding me with warnings and messages.

"Get on with ya."

"Save yourself."

"Get out while you can."

"You'll die here."

The urgency of their warnings forced me to act as I put Abigail's plan into action. I shuffled my way past the dim and empty nurse's station until I got to the door at the end of the hallway. I tried to push my way through, but it wouldn't give. A fresh wave of panic pulsed through me.

"Push harder."

I spun around, recognizing the little blond girl's voice right away, but I didn't see her. Even my ghostly companions had disappeared. *Come on,* I said to myself. *Get it together.* Putting all my weight into it, I slammed into the door. Sharp pain zapped my chest, my vision went black, and I tumbled into the stairwell. Once through, the door slammed shut behind me, but not before I heard shouting coming from the hallway I had just left. *Crap.* I wrapped my arms around my upper body and started down the stairs. With each step more painful than the last, I finally made it to the ground floor and to another door with a red sign that read, EMERGENCY EXIT ONLY. My options were clear. Go through the door that might trigger an alarm and trust that somehow Abigail would help me, or get caught in the hospital.

I pressed my forehead against the frame. The cold air from outside had chilled the wood. I was letting myself feel the coolness for a few seconds so I could catch my breath when the door jerked open from the other side. A shrill bell sounded, and I found myself face to face with my ambulance driver. I half collapsed into his arms.

"Come on," Roland muttered, holding me up and leading me to his ambulance. "Before they find us."

Roland and his son practically carried me to their ride, and the three of us crammed into the front seat with me in the middle. Without them on each side of me, I didn't think I'd be able to sit upright. I pulled my hands away from my chest and saw blood.

"Dad, he's bleeding!"

"I see it, Matthew."

I needed to go some place safe where I could get help. My great grandparents, Carmen and Julio, and their house close to Rice, sprang to mind. With their aid I might even be able to get back to my own time with Dominique and the others. Every time travel movie I had ever seen replayed in my mind. If I could get a message to Dominique, then maybe, just maybe, in the realm of all things even remotely possible, I could connect with my friends and get back home.

"Rice University," I said. "Please. I have family near there."

Somehow, through the searing pain in my chest, I managed to direct my getaway drivers to the small one-story house of my ancestors. When we pulled up, Carmen and Julio were outside waiting for me, as if they had known I was coming. With Roland's help, I managed to get inside and ended up on the bed that Dominique had lain on while Carmen banished Tavion's spirit.

Carmen went to work right away and started cutting off my shirt, but I needed to get my message to Dominique before it was too late. I grabbed Carmen's wrist. "I need a pen and paper," I said. *"Pluma y papel."*

"Pen and paper?" Matthew asked. "Why?"

"I don't know," Roland answered.

Sirens blared in the distance, and I knew it was only a matter of time before those officers would find me. *"¡Pluma y papel! ¡Por favor!"*

Julio left me on the cot, darted to the kitchen, and came back with what I wanted. I scribbled on the piece of paper. Too pained to translate my request to my great grandparents, I handed the paper to Roland.

"This message needs to get to my grandmother. In the future."

Roland frowned, a look of confusion on his face. I clung on to the sleeve of his perfectly pressed navy suit and jerked, my blood smearing on the fabric. "Please."

Roland opened the message and read it out loud. "This is Trent. I'm alive and stuck in Houston in 1930. Find Dominique and tell her."

Chapter Eight

~ Infiniti ~

Fleet had settled into a wicker chair in the corner in full man-spread mode.

"What's the deal with guys like you who sit like that?" I asked through a mouthful of hot Cheetos. I chased the glob of spicy goodness with a swig of the sweet wine. It wasn't the perfect combo, and I probably should've grabbed some chocolate instead, but it still hit the spot. Wiping my mouth, I added, "Is it a sign of having huge man parts, or is it all for show?"

I raised my eyebrow at him. "Well?" I took another chug of wine. "Do you have the goods or don't you?"

"Very funny, Tiny," Fleet said, closing his legs a little.

I busted out in laughter, forgetting about my troubles, and thoroughly enjoying my time taunting my crabby chaperon.

He got up, sauntered over to me, and held out his hand for a drink. I formed my lips into the shape of an O. "You want to join me? Finally?"

"Well," he said, "I've got nothing better to do."

I passed him the bottle and tossed him a bag of Cheetos. "Welcome to the party, pal. We may as well get used to being together, I guess."

"Yeah."

Crackling and popping from the fire filled the air while we passed the bottle back and forth and munched out. After a while, I started to get a little ADHD crazy. I got up and stretched my arms. "Let's see what we can find."

"Knock yourself out," Fleet said.

Moving through the nearly empty house, my mind replayed the images of my crying mom and Trent's desperate-looking grandmother. Then I thought of how Farrell had turned from Dominique's protector to deadly assassin and I wondered how Fleet felt about all that since they were brothers.

After finishing my self-guided tour and finding nothing of interest, I rejoined Fleet by the fire. "What's the deal with you and your brother?" I took a big drink. "Now that he has to, you know, kill us since we're on Dominique's side." With a hiccup, I opened a fresh bag of junk food. "Do you think you can stop him?" I handed him the bottle, but he waved it away. "Can you take him?"

Fleet ran his fingers through his dark hair. "You talk too much."

I finished the bottle with a series of swigs and opened the other. "He looks maybe" — I brought my hand up and left a little space between my thumb and forefinger — "a wee bit stronger than you." I covered my mouth, worried about hurting Fleet's feelings, but then broke out into laughter. "I'm sorry, Fleet. I couldn't help it. It was the wine speaking."

"Next time we see him, I'm gonna offer you up."

I bolted upright and a Cheeto fell out of my mouth. "You wouldn't!"

His deadpan face stretched into a grin. "Keep it up and I will."

If I had a pillow, I would've thrown it at him. "You jerk."

"Yeah, that's me."

He folded his arms and studied the ceiling, and immediately I felt bad for him. Like maybe he was a decent guy after all and not the jerk that Dominique and I had pegged him for. Suddenly, I wanted to really know him. Figure him out. "So what's your story, Fleet?"

"My story?"

"Yeah, back at the rest stop, Mrs. Wells apologized to you for everything. And on the road you asked your brother why he did it." I settled myself back on the couch and crisscrossed my legs, eager to hear Fleet's side of the story, sipping my cheap wine. "What gives?"

Howling wind whistled through the chimney. The gusts picked at the tongues of fire, taunting the flames until they grew tall with anger. As if sensing their conflict, Fleet sat up, his shoulders tense and on alert.

"Well?" I whispered.

He took hold of the armrests of his chair, as if bracing himself for a roller coaster ride, and said, "When I volunteered to infiltrate Tavion's ranks, I never knew it'd end up like this... my own people believing I had really turned, losing everyone I ever cared about. None of this was supposed to happen."

His tone had softened. His eyes were lost in his memories. I filled my mouth with wine and handed him the bottle. He took a long drink and then passed it back.

"The mission was for me to gather intel, find Tavion's weakness. But when he killed Dominique in her first life, and then again in her second, that's when I knew I was in it for the long haul. We all were. There would be no quick answer. No in-and-out James Bond solution. And as the lifetimes went on, and Dominique started losing her memories, everyone lost faith in me."

"Lost faith?"

He stuck his hand out for the bottle and downed the liquid. "Seems my acting skills had everyone fooled, even the people who sent me in."

"So that's why Mrs. Wells apologized," I muttered, taking the wine bottle back. "They thought you had turned. For real."

"I lost everything."

"How awful," I said. "To be abandoned like that. No wonder you're so pissed all the time. It's like losing your family, your best friend, heck, even your true love."

A flicker of pain flashed across his face, and that's when I knew what he meant when he had confronted Farrell and asked him why he had done it. My jaw dropped. "You and Dominique. You love her."

He practically jerked the bottle out of my grasp and took a swig. "None of it matters anymore."

I wanted to probe him about Dominique and find out more, but his tone and his stare warned me to let it go. "Fine, but I don't believe that it doesn't matter," I declared, taking back my bottle and shaking it to see how much was left. I took a small sip to conserve my dwindling supply. "Now what?"

"Finish the mission. Save Dominique. No matter what."

"Even if you have to kill your own brother?"

"If that's what it takes."

"Whoa, Fleet, you're like the Terminator dude." I forgot about conserving supplies and took a big, long chug of the sweet liquid, not even tasting the alcohol anymore, and then let out a deep burp. I slapped my hands over my mouth, and then burst out into laughter. "That was awesome!"

He chuckled. "I guess."

"Save Dominique, my frensh." A loud hiccup popped out of mouth. "I meansh friend. F-R-E-N-D," I spelled. My mind raced with ideas, and I latched onto one. I thought of the psychic cards Jan had given me and the Ouija board we had played. "I gots it!"

"You got what?"

I tried to tap my head, but missed and tapped my chin. "Evershing started when Dominique played my cards and used my shouija board."

Fleet looked at me as if I were a lunatic. And maybe I was a little, but I didn't care. I gulped my wine. "We deshtroy them, we deshtroy the magic." I collided my hands together and made a long raspberry sound with my lips, followed by a loud pop.

Fleet shook his head. "That won't do anything."

Untangling my legs, I leaped to my feet. My head spun. The room started swaying. "Ish better th-th-than nuthin."

I didn't even realize that Fleet was up too and holding my shoulders. I grabbed his shirt with my hands and pulled, and hiccuped. "Pleashe."

"You're dunk."

"I shnow."

My forehead started to burn, my mouth filled with saliva, my legs buckled. Fleet scooped me up and before I knew it, I was barfing into the kitchen sink. He held my long hair back, while my head hung over the stainless steel and a stream of orange chunks and red acid blasted out of me. I closed my eyes, not wanting to see the bile, the stench sharp and sour, my stomach lurching again and again and again.

When my gut finally relaxed, Fleet lifted me and placed me on the couch. "Houshton," I begged. "Deshtroy. Cards. Board." His boots thudded away and then thudded back. He draped something cool across my forehead. Guilt and remorse for coaxing Dominique into dabbling in the supernatural brought tears to my eyes. I thought of my crying mom, my house, my room, and all my things. Would I ever see them again?

"Pleashe. Fleet. Houshton."

"Okay," he said, wiping my face. "We'll go to Houston, Tiny."

Chapter Nine

~ Dominique ~

My fingertips trembled against my mouth, and my mind worked to process everything. How could I have fallen for Farrell if Fleet was my first love? Why didn't my parents tell me about our relationship with Tavion? I paced back and forth in front of the fireplace. "Is there anything else?"

Jake tapped his fingers on his legs. "Well, there's the little stuff like you and I dating for a spell, the hardships on your family when your dad denounced his brother, and one other small thing."

My fingers hesitated against my cracked lips. "What small thing?"

He examined me with sympathetic eyes and made me sit on the couch. "Well, as you know, Farrell is determined to kill you, right?"

"Right," I mumbled.

"He'll kill anyone and everyone to make that happen." He cleared his throat. "Thing is, if he's successful, he won't stop with you."

My brain couldn't compute what Jake had said. "What?"

"Dominique, he's warped now. If he ends you, he'll

66

continue his warpath until every last Pure is dead and the race is extinguished. What's left of us, that is, and there aren't that many." Jake rubbed my leg. "I'm really sorry, Dom."

He eased up from the couch, leaving me alone to deal with the aftermath of the bombshell he had dropped. While he rummaged through cabinets and drawers, the puzzle pieces of my life fell into place. I finally knew what my parents had meant when they said my death would doom our kind. "I have to live, then," I said. "No matter what. And the only way to do that is to kill Farrell. Even if I love him," I muttered mostly to myself.

Farrell... I had fallen in love with him even though I had been with Fleet in first life. No wonder Fleet hated me.

Jake placed a paper plate on my lap with a sandwich and chips. Peanut butter, by the smell of it. Even though I had said I wasn't hungry, my stomach started screaming for the food.

I took a small bite and chewed quietly.

"Look, Dom," Jake said. "I'm not the best at emotions and feelings and all that. It's not my thing. Okay?"

The dry bread scraped my throat as it went down. "What is your thing?"

His face lit up. "Action." He brought out the note I had written that said to kill Farrell. "Solutions. Survival."

I studied my handwriting. "Why would I write that in first life?"

Jake grabbed my hand and squeezed as if trying to make me feel better. "I have no idea, but you must've known he'd turn, and that you'd have to kill him."

Groaning, I let my head fall back on the cushion, but was met with a hard surface. "Ouch!" I rubbed the spot, swatting away Jake's attempts at wanting to examine my skull.

"Are you okay?" he asked with a half laugh.

"No," I said, referring to my heart more than my head. Even though Farrell had turned against me, he still filled my very soul. Yet I knew, without a doubt, that I had to kill him. It was either him or me and the entire race of Pures. "I guess I need time to process."

"Now that is a luxury we do have. With these collars on, we're completely safe and we can take all the time you need before we figure out our next move." He fumbled through a basket on the coffee table and held up the TV remote. "Let's find a good movie."

He pushed every button on the small clicker, but it wouldn't turn on. "Dumb TV," he grumbled, pressing harder with each passing second.

"Try the buttons down there." I pointed to the receiver in a black cabinet under the TV, my mind suddenly eager to escape my dismal reality.

Jake got on his hands and knees, opened the glass case, and started fiddling with the device. In no time, the screen brightened with images of the local news.

"And now, more on the story of the missing Texas teens and the nationwide manhunt to find them."

I jumped to my feet as photos of Trent and Infiniti flashed across the screen. A blond reporter stood outside Harmony High with a throng of students and parents behind her. A mound of flowers and candles were piled by the school entrance.

"With still no word on the whereabouts of missing teen Trent Avila, we are just now learning of footage from a gas station near Grand Rapids, Michigan and cell phone video from an incident nearby on Highway 75 that show seventeen-year-old Infiniti Clausman with her alleged abductor."

The screen switched to a video from inside the gas station I had run away from. Fleet stood near the entrance of the store. The cashier and a security guard had their guns drawn on him. Infiniti crouched on the ground. Flashing sparks emitted from Fleet's hands, and then the footage turned to crackling static.

"We're going to replay that video," the reporter said. "It appears the kidnapper has some sort of dangerous and possibly lethal electrical weapon in his hands."

The video replayed, paused, and then zoomed in on Fleet. Tall, with striking dark features and dark clothes, he looked more ominous than any movie villain I had ever seen.

"Shit," whispered Jake.

"And now," the reporter continued, "here's cell phone video captured mere hours ago that has exploded all over social media."

A hazy and shaky nighttime video appeared of people standing with their phones up, recording from the side of the highway. Fleet marched to Infiniti, yanked her arm, and said, "Come on." The image dropped to the street and showed legs and shoes as police sirens wailed and bullets fired.

"The hunt is on for the kidnapper the Internet has dubbed 'Hot Death.' If anyone has seen this brown SUV" — cell video of the speeding jeep flashed across the scene — "you are advised to use extreme caution and call the authorities right away."

The newscast returned to the lead anchor, who asked the reporter, "Are there any other leads in this case?"

"Not at the moment, and —"

"*¡Espera!*" a voice called from the crowd. "Wait!" Trent's grandmother approached the reporter, her cloudy eyes looking frantic and wild. "I have something to say!"

The surprised blonde moved closer to the matriarch. "Joining us is Mrs. Avila, grandmother of missing teen Trent Avila. Trent was last seen with Infiniti Clausman here in Houston at Harmony High about a week ago. Mrs. Avila..." Her voice lowered an octave. "What would you like to say?" She placed the microphone in front of Abuela's tired and worn face.

The small woman drew in a deep breath before staring straight at the camera. Her gaze sent a cascade of goose bumps across my body. "Dominique, *mija,* come see me."

Abuela walked away, and the reporter fumbled over her words before getting out, "We'll get back to you as this story develops."

Jake turned off the TV and stared at me. "What the—?"

I started pacing the room, talking out loud and trying to make sense of what I had just seen. "The authorities think Fleet kidnapped Infiniti. And Abuela wants to see me," I mumbled. "But why?"

Jake studied me, giving me space to sort through it all. I started thinking of Trent's bond with his grandmother and how she could sense things. That's when I knew. "It's Trent! He must be alive!" I could barely contain my excitement, suddenly eager to rush out of the house.

"Wait, what?"

"We left him for dead in the past, but he must be alive. Why else would his grandmother want to see me?"

Jake rubbed his head. "I guess, but what about this whole Fleet kidnapping Infiniti thing? I thought you said he was on our side."

"He is," I declared, suddenly seeing Fleet in a new light. "He and Infiniti must've somehow gotten separated from my mom. I have no idea what the media thinks is going on, but I know Infiniti will be okay with Fleet. Right now we need to see Trent's grandmother. It's our first real clue."

"Okay."

His lack of hesitation surprised me. "Really?"

"Really. This is our call to action. But we leave in the morning, okay? At first light. It's too dark and too damn cold. Plus, we have no transportation."

The day was long gone and night had settled in without me even realizing it. I peered through the wood blinds and couldn't see a thing through the dark.

"Wanna make the most of things before we set out tomorrow? Maybe relax a little and do some stargazing?" Jake asked. "We used to all the time."

I closed the blinds and studied him. Tall and lanky, a little on the nerdy side, I wondered if I could trust him. He did seem to know a lot about me. "We really dated?"

He laughed. "Yep. But we were young. We only held hands," he said, looking sheepish.

Still worked up about what I had seen on the news, but knowing full well that we needed daylight before setting out, I pulled the blanket from the sofa and draped it over my shoulders. "Fine, let's go outside for a bit."

The whipping wind from earlier had died down, yet the piercing cold remained. Jake wrapped his arm around me and drew me in as we gazed out over the deck. The dark sky sparkled with a million stars. The roaring, white-capped waves crashed in and rushed out. Tiny lights flickered way out in the distance. For a few seconds, I thought of staying on this island and hiding out forever, but I knew I couldn't. Too many had died for me, and I couldn't let that be for nothing.

"Hey," Jake said. "Do you want to know more about first life? I can fill you in. At least from my perspective."

Mom, Dad, and Farrell had kept my past lives a secret. At first I was angry at them for doing that, but now I understood. I wasn't that person anymore. I was different. Changed forever. Besides, I wasn't going that way. My path lay ahead of me, not behind me.

"I know everything I need to know."

"That's probably best," Jake said. He let the quiet descend on us for a minute before he said, "Let's see what's up there."

He led me across the deck and to a set of stairs I hadn't noticed in the dark. Step by step, we climbed up to a square-shaped landing, like a lookout at the top of a castle. The entire Gulf was spread out like a majestic backdrop. "Wow," I said with a soft exhale, feeling as if I was standing on top of the world. "It's beautiful up here."

"Sure is."

My body started shivering and Jake drew me even closer. As I gazed over the railing, a warm heat emanated from him, almost as if he were a man-sized space heater. I looked up at him. "How are you doing that?"

"I'm magnifying my body heat," he said. "It's one of the rare perks of the trade."

"Rare?" I asked, thinking that being able to manipulate energy was probably a cool skill to have. "What do you mean?"

He leaned over, keeping his gaze glued on the ocean scene. "It's tough being a Transhuman in a world where we're a dying breed." He paused for a long while. "Sometimes I wish I was like everyone else. Life would be a lot easier."

My hand traveled to the back of my neck, to the mark that Tavion had placed there when I was born, and I immediately sympathized with Jake. I never asked to be different, never wanted to be the Marked One. Yet here I was, fighting for my life. Again. If I could choose another life, I would.

Jake rubbed his hands together and gave me a smile. "Enough serious talk," he said. "Let's sit."

Two Adirondack chairs were stacked in the corner. Her pulled them apart, took my hand, and we sat. Still unsure about him, I started to draw my hand away, but he wouldn't let me. "If you want to stay warm, you need to hold on."

My hand twitched in his, and doubts about him sprang to mind. Especially after everything I'd been though. He held on tight and leaned toward me. "Dom, we *are* best friends. I promise." Breakers roared in the distance, the cold air tickled my face. "You can trust me," he whispered.

"Can I?"

"Yes. You can."

Desperate to have someone to lean on now that I had lost everyone I ever cared about, I let my grip relax in his palm. Shrouded in silence, my mind replayed the images I had seen on the news when a repeating whistle-like noise sounded in the air.

Jake dropped my hand and got to his feet. Joining him at the wooden railing of the landing, we peered out in the distance. Red flashing lights dotted the road. Blinking closer to us, the signal grew to wail.

"The cops," I warned, terrified of being thrown in jail for breaking and entering. And then I remembered I was supposed to be dead, burnt to a crisp in a car accident. "We need to get out of here."

"Exactly," Jake agreed, pulling me to the stairs. "Come on."

We had started to bound down the stairs, when Jake

stopped. "Shit, my backpack," he said. He darted into the house and came back with his pack strapped to this back. Pulling me, we raced to the ground floor. With each step, the flashing lights and blaring siren grew nearer.

"There," Jake said. He dashed to a garage door, but it was locked. He gave it a kick and muttered under his breath.

I surveyed our options, only one real choice ahead of us: hide on the beach. "This way," I said, starting for the wooden walkway that went over the dunes, when the crunching sound of tires over sand filled the air. Headlights lit up the concrete driveway, and a car rolled up. Not a police car, but a black Jeep. Jake and I backed up into the darkness and hid behind an outdoor shower stall. Two car doors opened.

"Bert, honey, let's wait for the police," a woman said.

"That's probably best," the man grumbled. "Damn vagrants."

"I know, honey."

The police sped up the drive, screeching to a halt behind the jeep. "Ma'am, sir, get back in your vehicle and lock the doors while we search the premises."

The cops thudded up the stairs. Jake jerked his chin in the direction of the Jeep. "There's our ride."

Chapter Ten

~ Trent ~

With my head nestled in a soft pillow, and my body relaxed and pain free, I slipped into a dreamy state, not fully knowing where I was and yet not exactly caring. It was the kind of rest halfway to slumber that stretched out into an immeasurable space.

"*Trent*," a soft voice whispered.

My brain worked to wake my body so I could answer the girl, but it wouldn't listen to me.

"*Trent*." Something soft, like hair, bristled at my ear. "*She got your message*."

***

My eyelids parted. The shabby but comfortable house of my ancestors came into view, fuzzy at first, but clearer with each blink. Streaks of light poured into the room. My great-grandmother, Carmen, kept watch by my side. I sat up, and she handed me a glass of water. After gulping it down, I scanned the open area.

"You're up."

I started to turn in the direction of the voice, but a sharp pain in my upper body stopped me.

"Careful." It was the guy from the ambulance, coming into the cramped room. "Don't move so fast."

Carmen grunted her disapproval at his approach, so he stopped. "Your" — he motioned at Carmen, not knowing how to refer to her — "friend wanted me to sit out in the living room. She's very protective of you."

"Her name is Carmen," I offered. "And you're... Matthew?"

"Yes, and you're Trent?" He approached me with a shaky outstretched hand that Carmen smacked away with lightning speed.

"Carmen," I said. *"Es okay. Es un amigo."*

She slowly returned to her seat, but kept a sharp eye on Matthew, who rubbed his hand before lowering it. I couldn't help but laugh. "She's pretty strong, isn't she?"

"Yes, she is."

With a grunt, I started to sit up. Matthew made a move to help, but Carmen blocked him like a defensive basketball player and placed a row of pillows behind me for support.

"Sorry, man," I said to Matthew, giving in to Carmen's watchful ways.

"It's okay."

I lifted the sheet from my body and noticed a fresh layer of gauze around my chest. The smell of minty vapor drifted up to me, clearing my head.

"She re-stitched your wound," Matthew explained. "After you passed out."

"I see." I nodded at her. *"Gracias."*

She nodded back, and an awkward silence fell on the room.

"So, where is everyone?" I asked. I didn't see my great-grandfather, Julio, or his brother Javier, or Matthew's dad.

Matthew rubbed his hands on his crisp uniform pants and tugged at his buttoned collar. Nervous? Warm? I couldn't tell. "The two men who live here left this morning, dressed for gardening. My father is with the coppers, making a statement."

My face must've taken on a paranoid expression because Matthew held out his hand as if to calm me. "It's okay," he offered. "It's routine questioning. They saw us drive away from the hospital around the time you escaped last night, but they didn't see us take you."

My racing heartbeat slowed some, but I was still scared. Those cops were out there looking for me, and I knew they wouldn't give up that easily. I rubbed my face, trying to figure out my next move. My great-grandmother narrowed her dark eyes and tilted her head, studying me with a worry-filled stare.

"Are you," Matthew paused, "really from the future?"

The note I had written. Of course. Now Matthew's nervous body language made sense.

"You're not crazy, are you?" he asked, stepping away from me a little, a look of awe mixed with horror on his face.

Matthew and I were the same age, but he was from the 30s, the dark time of the Great Depression where people had very little hope and a whole lot of suspicion. Especially Hispanics. Matthew and his dad could lose their jobs over helping me, maybe even end up in jail. I had to be careful with my words because I needed allies here if I was ever going to make it back home—if that was even possible.

"I'm not crazy. But you're right. I'm not exactly from here. Let's wait for your dad to come back, and then I'll explain everything to both of you."

With Carmen's help, I got out of bed, cleaned up as much as possible without aggravating my stitches, and even had a bite to eat. Dressed in a fresh pair of jeans and a plaid long-sleeve shirt, I did my best to patiently wait for the others to return.

After a few hours of awkward small talk and curious glances from Matthew, an urgent knock sounded at the door. "It's me. Roland. *Abra la puerta.*"

Carmen opened the door right away, letting Roland in along with a gust of frigid air. He rubbed his hands together. "That Mother has it in for ya, kid."

My hopes for making it out of this century sank, capsized by an overzealous nun and her obsession with finding me. "She does?"

Roland took off his uniform hat and rubbed his short cropped hair. "She's believes you're either the devil or possessed by the devil. She even has the chief convinced, and he's started a city-wide manhunt for your capture." Roland gave me a hard look. "Look, kid, if you want my help, you need to come clean with me. See? I can't stick my neck out for ya if I don't know what I'm up against."

Carmen placed a hand on my shoulder. I could tell she wanted me to translate what Roland had said, so I did. When I finished, she put her hand on my cheek. *"Confiar en él."*

She wanted me to trust him?

"Kid, listen to your lady friend," he said. "You can trust me." His face softened. "Those nuns are hell bent on finding you, and I gotta feeling you're innocent."

My chest started burning. The room swayed. Sensing my pain, Carmen latched onto my arm and led me to the kitchen table. She poured me a glass of water and handed me two white pills, telling me they would help ease my discomfort. I downed them, then waited for Roland and Matthew to join us.

"I'll explain everything, but first I need to know why you're doing this for me. You don't even know me." I thought of my home, my *abuela*, my friends, and almost started to choke up, but stopped myself. "Why are you helping me?"

"Kid," Roland said, unbuttoning the top gold button of his jacket. "Trent. You're what, seventeen?"

Roland and Matthew were dressed in their navy ambulance attire, but didn't have their hats on in the house. They looked like sensible, upstanding citizens. I wondered how much of my story they'd believe. "Yes, sir."

"That's Matthew's age." He rubbed his forehead, his gaze stopping on his son for a minute before returning to me. "I tell you right now, if my boy were ever in a situation where he was shot and alone, I'd want someone to step up for him. See? Especially against the accusations of a white church in a town run by white people."

I was beginning to think getting back to my century was the least of my problems.

"Now let's hear it." Roland pulled the note I had written out of his pocket, placed it on the table, and tapped it with his finger. "Explain."

The pain in my chest had spread out across my upper body, and I wondered how long it would take the medicine to work. Forcing myself not to think about my wound, I was wracking my brain for the right words, when my focus went to their tan skin. They were Hispanic, like me, so they had to have some understanding and maybe even a little belief in the concept of otherworldly things since our heritage was filled with superstition.

"Okay," I said, clearing my throat. "Before I begin, I

need you to know I'm not crazy." I focused on Matthew, and then on Roland. "I'm not. But what I'm about to tell you may be hard to believe." I blew out a deep breath. "But it's all true, I promise."

Roland shifted in his seat. "Go on."

"On second thought," I said. "Let me show you." I held out my palm, willing my aura to appear, my hand shaking from effort, but nothing happened. I dropped my arm. "It's not working."

Matthew and Roland scooted away from me, confusion and fear on their faces. "What's not working?" Roland asked.

I knew I needed a different approach fast before they took me to the cops themselves. "Never mind," I said. "Let me just tell you straight."

"Okay," Roland said.

"You know how a *curandero* or *curandera* can work with the spirits and knows things and can even heal people, right?"

Roland and Matthew nodded.

"Well, there's these people that are a lot like that called Transhumans." I thought of Farrell and Fleet and the others and how they were able to manipulate energy. I also thought about being a Supreme, and the power that I was able to command but for whatever reason couldn't produce anymore. "These people can do things with their minds. They have these"—I stumbled over my words before finding the right one—"powers."

"Like in the comics?" Matthew asked.

"Yes! Like that!" I said, hopeful for the first time and thinking that maybe explaining everything wouldn't be so hard.

The dad raised his eyebrow, but didn't say anything.

"These people had a huge fight and split into two groups, the Pure and the Tainted. After a really long time of fighting, they decided to let everything ride on one life. A girl. Dominique. She's my friend." A jab of pain stabbed at my chest, not because of my injury, but because Dominique had taken over my heart. She was still there even though she loved someone else, and I had no idea what was happening to her or if she was even alive.

Roland leaned in. "What do you mean?"

"Whoever kills her, wins," I whispered.

"What kind of people would do that?" Matthew asked.

"Gangsters," the dad sneered.

"Yeah, they're like gangsters. Really strong and deadly gangsters. My friends and I, and Dominique, were in the middle of a fight with them, when..." My voice trailed off, the image of being in the church flooded my mind—the swirling electrical current that came from me and Farrell, the nuns that barged into the sanctuary. I could almost smell the lingering incense from the place, could almost feel the heat of the sparkling vapor in my hands. I grasped the edges of the table and steadied myself. "There was this electrical storm, and my friends and I were almost home when the Mother Superior and her nun found us. My friends actually made it back, but I got stuck here when the sister shot me."

"So your friends are home? You didn't kill anyone?" Matthew asked, his questions laced with relief.

"That's right, I did not kill anyone."

The dad eyed his son, and then he zeroed in on me. "Trent, kid, where is home so we can help you get there?"

"That's the thing," I said, the pain in my upper body starting to numb from the pills. "I'm from Houston. But... from the future."

The front door flew open. A little boy around five years old burst into the house, followed by Julio and Javier. The child ran to Carmen's side, staring at us wide-eyed, and I knew exactly who it was because I had seen his picture before. It was my grandfather.

"*¡Ya vienen!*" My great-grandfather warned, hurrying over to the kitchen table. "No safe."

"They're coming? Who?" I said, all of us alert and on our feet.

"*¡La policía!*"

"They said they wouldn't search the campus area until tomorrow. Damn that Danny," Roland muttered, securing his hat on his head. "Matthew, take Trent out the back door and make tracks. Get him to the house. Hide out until I get there, and don't answer the door for nobody. I'll stay in the area and run interference."

"Yes, sir," Matthew said, retrieving his hat.

I grabbed the note from the table and shoved it into Carmen's rugged hands, telling her to save it and give it to my grandfather when he was older. I knew she wouldn't let me down because the voice from my dreams told me that Dominique had received my message. With the paper in hand, she nodded, kissed my cheek, and then pulled me in for a tight hug. "*Vaya con Dios, Trenius.*"

My gaze lingered on her tear-filled eyes for a second before I bent down in front of my five-year-old grandfather. When I did, I spotted a chain around his neck with a dark cross. When I cupped it in my hand, a warm vibration tickled my skin. It was the cross Abigail had given him after she died at Julian Huxley's house that my grandmother later gave to Dominique. I had used it to save her in the red desert.

"Trent, Matthew, get on with ya," Roland warned. "Now."

I ruffled the little boy's head. "Don't lose this, okay?" I gazed up at Carmen. *"Es muy importante. Es para mi amiga, Dominique."*

"Come on," Matthew urged, steering me away from my family and out the back door. This time I knew I wouldn't be returning. I'd either find my way back home, or end up in jail.

The cold February air nipped at my face as I followed Matthew around to the side of house and to an old, rusty motorcycle.

"For real?" I asked.

Matthew narrowed his eyes and gave me a questioning look. "Yes, that bike is real. Now let's go."

He hopped on the narrow seat that wasn't nearly long enough for two people, and edged up as far as he could. Grumbling, but knowing I had no other option, I sidled up behind him and we took off.

The high-pitched wailing of police sirens sounded in the distance. With my arms cradling my ribs for support, and the image of my grandfather's cross in my mind, the cross that would eventually be gifted by Abuela to Dominque, an idea struck me. When I first got here with Dominique, Infiniti, and Farrell, we thought it was because we needed to find Professor Julian Huxley. Instead, we found my ancestors and with their help expelled the Tainted out of Dominique. With that behind us, and with me stuck here, maybe *I* needed to see Huxley. What if he could help me get home? He was the one who had studied Abigail after all. I didn't see that necklace for nothing. It had to be a sign.

Question was, could I find the professor before the cops found me?

Chapter Eleven

~ Infiniti ~

A pounding crashed against my skull like a sledgehammer. A thick, fuzzy film covered my tongue and teeth. "What the hell," I muttered, peering about the wood-paneled room from a pile of blankets and pillows.

"You got drunk."

Fleet's voice shook my brain and I covered my ears. "Shhhh," I said, in a low voice. "Geez, whisper." I clamped my eyes shut, trying to steady my throbbing head.

"Give me your hand, Tiny. I've got coffee."

"Thank God." I flung my arm out and wiggled my fingers, desperate for a dose of caffeine.

He placed his warm hand on my small and cold one, guiding it to the heated cup. With a shaky arm, I brought the mug to my mouth. The warmth against my lips felt good, as did the hot liquid sliding down my throat. "Ahhh, thanks."

I handed the cup back to him and eased myself back down on the bed. Through a cracked eyelid, I noticed the blinds were raised. Sunlight poured into the rustic room, the bright light sending pangs of discomfort through my temples. I shielded my eyes with my hand. "Can you close that?"

"Nope," he says. "We gotta move. Staying in one place too long is dangerous."

With a soft groan, I flipped onto my stomach and buried my face in the fabric. The sour stink of feet assaulted me, and a splash of burning vomit came up in my throat. With a swallow, I rolled over to my back again, escaping the foulness. "Ughhhhh. I just threw up in my mouth."

"Come on," he urged. "Let's move."

"I'm in pain here!"

The bed creaked under his weight as he sat beside me. His fingers pressed against my forehead. I swatted at his arm "What are you doing?"

He pressed harder. "Helping."

A pleasant vibration oozed connected at my skin, but faded away fast. He pulled his hand way. "Dammit," Fleet muttered. "I thought it might work. Sorry."

"I'm doomed to be miserable." I moaned, regretting drinking all that wine.

He laughed, getting up from the bed and standing by the door. "Doomed or not, you have five minutes."

Most days I hated my out-of-control hair. But now, on the run from the cops and dealing with a killing machine like Farrell, it was nice to not worry about my crazy curls. Added bonus, the cabin's bathroom was fully stocked with deodorant, toothpaste, and a toothbrush—every girl's best friend after a night of retching. And even, hallelujah, a small bottle of ibuprofen.

After getting myself together as best as I could, I joined Fleet in the den. "Remind me to never drink red wine and stuff my face with hot Cheetos ever again."

Fleet made his way to the front door. "Don't drink red wine and stuff your face with hot Cheetos ever again. Now let's go."

"Smart ass," I said with a growl, following him outside. The brilliant sun couldn't warm the frigid air, but it did blind me for a few seconds. When my vision adjusted to the outside, I noticed our car had changed. Instead of the beat-up Jeep that Richard had let us borrow, a red van awaited us.

I put my hand on my hip and stuck out my foot. "Seriously? A mom van?"

"After all those cell phones last night on the highway taking videos and pictures, I had to switch out the car."

"While I was passed out?"

"Yep."

"And you had to get *this*?"

"It'll allow you to rest in the back on our way to Houston," he said, climbing into the car.

My mouth fell open as I climbed in next to him and buckled up. "So that wasn't a dream? Asking you to take me to Houston and you saying yes?"

The car crunched through snow as we traveled away from the cabin and back to the highway. "It wasn't a dream."

I kept my stare on him, my mind trying to figure out why he'd follow any suggestion of mine. "Why did you listen to me? I mean, I'm glad you did, but why?"

The frigid car had started to warm. My body stopped shivering. Fleet looked like he didn't want to answer, but eventually he said, "I don't have any other ideas."

I sank back in my seat, numb. "*You* don't have any ideas? So now we're following mine? Great. We are so screwed."

"I wouldn't say that," he said. "A lot happened in Houston. Plus, I still have that journal from Professor Huxley. Going back there may give us clues."

He reached into his jeans pocket for what I thought was the journal, but he handed me a cell phone instead. I hungrily grabbed at it, missing mine since Dominique's mom forced us to give up our electronics for our own safety.

With an ooh and an aah, I rubbed my hands all over the device. "Where did you get this?"

"Doesn't matter. And no messing around on that," he ordered, stopping me before I went full-on social media crazy. "Just check the internet for news on the missing Texas teens. Nothing else."

"What? There are missing teens from Texas?"

He shot me a look. "Really?"

And then I remembered the newscast from the truck stop. I giggled. "Oh, me and Trent. Sorry."

Feeling really dumb, I focused on my task and typed in the search bar *Missing Texas Teens*. Before I clicked, I added *Infiniti Clausman* and *Trent Avila*. My fingers paused over the buttons of the phone. A pang of guilt over the loss of my friend stalled my hand for a second before I finished my action and tapped the search button. The screen filled with pages upon pages of news stories. I quickly scanned the top ones.

"Hot Death" Kidnapper Seen In Michigan With Missing Texas Teen

Shots Fired on Michigan Highway, "Hot Death" Speeds Away With Missing Teen

The Sexiest Kidnapper Alive? '"Hot Death" Seen in Michigan, Reward Offered

"Hot Death" Uses Handheld Electrified Weapon

"Holy Shit, we're all over the internet, and everyone is calling you the sexiest kidnapper alive." I clicked on a video of me and Fleet in the gas station, and then a video of our confrontation on the highway with Farrell and subsequent shootout with the cops. I held the phone in front of Fleet's face so he could see.

"Fucking great," he muttered, slamming his hands against the steering wheel.

"We are so famous," I whispered.

"It's the kind of famous we don't need."

"You're right," I said, feeling excited at first but then realizing that being tracked by the cops and maybe even most of America could put us in jeopardy with Farrell.

I kept scrolling the feed, when a totally different story caught my attention. *Distraught Grandmother of Missing Teen Makes Bizarre Statement.* I tapped on it right away, and saw a news reporter standing in front of Harmony. Trent's little old grandmother came through the crowd and said, "Dominique, *mija,* come see me."

My mouth dropped. My blood chilled.

"What?" Fleet asked. "What is it?"

"There's a clip on here of Trent's grandmother asking Dominique to come see her."

"Show me."

I leaned over and played the video, then waited for him to say something, but he didn't. Instead, he drove in silence, which killed me. Of course, I wanted to decipher the video to death. "Why do you think Trent's grandmother said that? Do you think Dominique got the message? Do you think she'll go to Houston?"

Fleet didn't respond to any of my prodding, and I wanted to punch him. "Hey! What do you think?"

"I think we're going to the right place at the right time."

"Seriously? That's all you have to say?" I tried to steady myself so I wouldn't say something I'd regret, wondering what happened to the cool guy who held my hair while I puked. "Listen, Fleet, I get that you're this unemotional guy who doesn't like to talk, but can we at least come up with a plan?"

"We don't need a plan right now."

Irritated at his stubbornness, I said, "Well, I think we do."

"Okay, come up with one then."

I knew he was trying to placate me, but I didn't care. We needed to figure out what we were going to do when we got to Houston. Plus, he had no idea who he was dealing with.

Kicking my feet up on the dashboard, I started a stream of consciousness monologue I knew would irritate the hell out of him. I babbled about Fran, the cards she had given me that sparked Dominique's visions, the Ouija board that helped Tavion find her, the trip to the past, my sorrow over losing Veronica and then Trent, the horror of seeing Dominique's decapitated dad, the fact that I was still a virgin and didn't know if I should try to get Billy back or not.

"Enough!" Fleet hollered, cutting me off before I could go on. "We go to your house, do that thing you said about destroying the cards and the board, see if that helps with anything, and then head to Trent's grandmother's. Okay?"

Crossing my arms with a smirk, satisfied that I had driven him to formulating a plan that aligned with what I wanted, I said, "Perfect!" Then I realized that I needed to pee. "Hey, I need to go to the bathroom."

A rest stop sprang to view as if on cue. We turned in and coasted to a parking spot at the far end of the lot. Luckily, it was early and the place looked empty. Fleet reached around to the backseat, grabbed a plastic bag, and tossed it on my lap. "Put this on."

"A bag? You want me to put on a bag?"

"No, what's inside the bag," he gritted out.

Sifting through the contents, I pulled out a plain, blue baseball cap and pair of reading glasses that had the lenses popped out. Gathering my hair up and putting on the hat and nerd frames, I turned to my driver. "How do I look?"

"Fine."

Not taking his word for it, I studied myself in the vanity mirror. "Where's your disguise?" I asked, tucking a few stray curls up into the cap.

"I'm going to say here and keep a lookout."

Fear crawled up into my throat, strangling me and taking my words. "Wh-wh-what? Don't you think I might need you in there?"

"You'll be fine. Now hurry."

Great. Some bodyguard. Slamming the car door behind me, I speed walked to the entrance, hurried across the convenience store, and made it to the bathroom without anyone looking at me. On the way out, passing the cashier who had his face buried in his phone, I glanced at the racks of junk food. My stomach lurched, and remorse over ruining my love for hot Cheetos forever settled in my gut.

Breaking out into the cool morning, relieved that I had made it in and out without incident, an uneasy feeling overcame me. I slowed my pace. As if sensing it too, Fleet climbed out of the van. The sky darkened. Bolts of lightning streaked across the heavens. Fleet zoomed to my side and grabbed my arm to haul me to the safety of our ride. But a flash of bright light blinded us, stopping us in our tracks. When it dissipated, Farrell appeared, a long, white staff in hand. My mouth fell open when I recognized the rod as Colleen's.

Fleet moved me behind him. "What did you do to her?" he asked, his tone cool and menacing.

Farrell raised the staff up, then slammed it on the ground. A green hue burst from the tip, spiraling up into the clouds before racing down and filtering into his mouth. His form lifted, the stream pulsed with power. When the surge had entered him completely, the staff disintegrated into a thousand little pieces of dust and floated away. "I ended her."

The guy from inside the store burst through the doors. "Hey, you guys, did ya see —?"

Farrell hurled a blast of energized matter at him, freezing him in place midsentence. Whipping my head around, I noticed that even the nearby cars travelling on the highway had stopped mid-motion. "What do you want?" I yelled.

He kept his stance wide, his glare on us. "Any leads on the whereabouts of the Marked One?"

"You mean your girlfriend who you used to care about?" I hurled my words at him, hoping they'd jar him from his murderous task, but knowing better. I tugged at Fleet's shirt and whispered, "Don't mention Houston."

"What's in Houston?" Farrell asked, coming closer to us.

"We have no leads, so we decided to go back to the beginning," Fleet offered, his hands fisted so tight I could see the whites of his knuckles while a thin vapor of power pulsed from his fingers.

"If we find anything, we'll call for you. Now leave us the hell alone!" I hollered.

Farrell sauntered closer, oozing with sexy danger. He stuffed his hand in his jeans pocket and pulled something out. "Don't double cross me."

He flung the small object at Fleet and then vanished. Catching the item with a swoop, Fleet held it up for inspection. I gasped when I saw the tiny bullet. It was the same one Mrs. Wells had dropped into her coat pocket.

"Oh my God," I whispered. "He killed her, too. Why?"

"She must've gotten in his way," Fleet said, his jaw clenching with rage.

"Hey," a voice called out. I turned to see that the store cashier had sprung back to life as well as the cars travelling the highway. "You guys almost got hit by that thunderbolt. You okay?"

Fleet ushered me to the van. "We're fine," he said with a wave. "Thanks."

For once in my life, I was too freaked to say anything. So we drove on in silence. Traveling from state to state, stopping sparingly, napping in the back, we inched closer to our destination.

Farrell had killed Colleen. He had ended Caris, Dominique's mom. He was on a murderous rampage, and we were probably next.

"I don't want to die," I confessed to Fleet.

"You won't."

Staring at the passing fields, I didn't believe him.

Chapter Twelve

~ Dominique ~

My nose dripped from the cold air and my fingers were chilled to the bone as Jake and I crept from our hiding spot behind the outdoor shower to the black Jeep. A gust of wind blew sand into my eyes, and I had to wipe my tears on my sleeve. Crouching low to the ground, we shuffled along the wall to the garage, inching closer to our soon-to-be getaway car parked on the cement driveway.

Before bursting from our cover, I pulled Jake back. "No one gets hurt."

"Of course."

On the count of three, we sprang out. The driver was an older man with a bald head and gray beard. Next to him sat a woman with a narrow, tan face, and short salt-and-pepper hair.

Jake pulled a gun from the back of his borrowed sweatpants and pointed it at the windshield. "Out! Now!"

"Jake," I whispered. "What the hell?"

"We don't have time to screw around," he muttered.

The couple, who must've been Bert and Joanne from Beaumont, slowly exited the vehicle, hands up over their heads. "Go ahead," the tiny woman said calmly. "Take the car. We don't want any trouble."

They moved out of our way as we approached, keeping their stares on us.

"You don't have to do this," the man offered. "We can help you. We know the DA and we can—"

"Shut up!" Jake yelled, thrusting his pistol in the man's face.

"Jake! Stop!" I jerked his sleeve. "No one gets hurt, remember?"

The woman eyed me curiously, then held her hand out to me. "Honey, you don't have to go with him if you don't want to." Her face took on a look, as if she felt sorry for me. She had no idea.

"I'm okay," I said, wondering for a second about the couple. Did they have kids? Grandkids? Did they spend holidays at the beach house? A sharp pang of homesickness for my family settled in my chest. Especially since I had caused the death of my dad. "I'm really sorry," I offered, suddenly feeling the need to apologize to them.

Arm in arm, the couple backed away. We hopped in the car and sped away from the house and down a dark two-lane highway. Jake kept his gaze on the rear-view mirror.

Relieved, yet irritated at the whole Wild West move, I punched his arm. "A gun? You have a gun?"

"Yeah, for emergencies."

"Why didn't you tell me?"

He shrugged. "It wasn't important."

He made a sharp right turn onto a road that lead to a cluster of homes, most of which looked empty and closed up for the winter. He slowed the car to a crawl and turned off the headlights. "We need a new ride," he said.

"You should've told me you had a gun," I pressed, still pissed at the way he had threatened that couple.

"Well, how did you think we were gonna get that car, huh? Say please?"

Crossing my arms and ignoring him, I thought Jake had a point. What *was* I thinking? As if the couple would have just handed over their keys?

He stopped next to a darkened house with a black truck in the driveway. "I'm sorry, Dom. I'm used to being alone, that's all," he explained, sounding a little sad. "I should've told you I had a gun."

"It's okay," I muttered, deciding to let him off the hook because I had no idea what he'd been through. I eyed the gigantic truck. "The cops will know we took the truck as soon as it's reported missing."

"Maybe. But by the looks of the house, everyone inside is asleep. Nobody will know the truck is gone until tomorrow."

Ditching Bert and Joanne's Jeep, Jake broke into the car with no problems. Using his Transhuman skills, he started the car and put it in neutral. I steered and he pushed until we were halfway out of the neighborhood. When he hopped in, we switched places and continued in the opposite direction of our short-lived safe place.

Thinking we were in the clear and wondering what had happened to the cops, sirens sounded in the distance. Red lights appeared on the road. My heart exploded against my ribs and my gut knotted.

"Be cool," Jake warned.

Slouching down in my seat, I peered at the side-view mirror. The dotted lights were getting smaller and smaller, the shrill of the sirens fading.

"They're not following us!" I blurted, thinking that for once something had gone my way. Sitting up, I watched the lights driving in the opposite direction.

"Weird," Jake said.

"Maybe Joanne and Bert took pity on us and sent them the wrong way."

"Maybe."

Relieved, but knowing the feeling wouldn't last, we traveled to the end of the road that merged into a ferry access. "Crap," Jake said, coming to a near halt. "Do we get on?"

The cops were long gone, but what if they had called the ferry operators and reported us? What if they had our physical descriptions? Even a big, black truck wouldn't hide us. "I don't know."

A honk sounded, jarring us to the reality that other drivers had lined up behind us. We now had no choice but to move ahead. Jake crawled forward in the car. "It'll be fine," he said. He took my hand and held it tight. "Just act casual."

His hold turned hot. Wisps of vapor trickled from him and inched up my arm. I wanted to jerk away, but he wouldn't let me. "What are you doing?"

"Disguising you."

A trail of warmth crawled up my skin, reaching all the way to the top of my scalp. The tingling sensation actually felt pretty good, like an amazing deep-tissue massage. When the tickling faded, I glanced at Jake and did a double-take. His hair had grown by at least three inches and was now jet black. He looked like the front man in an indie rock band.

"Whoa," I said, wondering what he had done to my appearance, my head still tickly.

Jake released his grip as we rolled up to a booth. He lowered his window. An elderly lady eyed us. "What was your business in Bolivar?"

"Vacation," Jake answered.

The woman looked down at her clipboard, and then motioned us forward. "Move along."

Driving away, I rubbed my head. "What did you do?"

"See for yourself."

I lowered the visor and saw that my long, brown hair had turned blond. My olive-colored eyes were a bright blue. And, I kinda liked it. "This is crazy."

Jake laughed. "I wasn't sure if I should do red or blond."

Stroking my new do, I asked, "How long will the color last?"

"A few hours."

We drove onto the ferry and were waved to the front of the flat boat. Turning our engine off, we waited while other vehicles lined up around us. Jake's leg bounced at a rapid pace, his gaze flicking from the rear-view mirror to the side mirror. My shoulders tightened. I sat on the edge of my seat, waiting not so patiently for the ferry to leave the dock.

"Come on," Jake said, tapping the steering wheel. "Let's go."

After what felt like hours, a loud foghorn blared and the hefty ferry churned forward. I blew out a sigh of relief, not even realizing I had been holding my breath. "Finally," I said.

Jake leaned his head back. "Yep, finally."

A surge of exhaustion came over me, and suddenly I could barely keep my eyes open. I snuggled into my seat. "I'm gonna close my eyes for a minute."

He folded his arms across his chest and relaxed his body. "Me too."

The stillness inside the truck calmed me. The soft

whistling of the wind against the windows eased my fears like a hypnotic suggestion.

"Hey," a voice said. "Dominique."

I shifted to my side, my cheek meeting a gritty and rough substance. *What?* I pried my heavy eyelids open and saw that I lay on sand. I sat up, sputtering out the grit that had seeped into my mouth, knowing exactly where I was— Elk Rapids beach, my safe haven with Farrell. But instead of a feeling of protection, fear gripped me.

"What's that around your neck?"

Fully awake now, and in absolute panic mode, I spun around to see Farrell. The last time we were here at this beach, he said he had to kill me and begged me to run. I jumped to my feet and backed away from him, my fingertips touching the metal choker around my neck, wondering why it wasn't working.

"How did you find me?"

"I didn't," he said, his face pained, his eyes full of regret. "This is a dream." He stepped closer, and I let him.

Looking down on me, he traced my cheek with his fingertips. A wave of desire coursed through me, and I melted inside. Even though he was my new enemy, even though I had to kill him, I still wanted him.

"That metal around your neck is keeping me from finding you, isn't it?"

"Yes," I whispered. "It is." Losing control of myself and giving into my desire, I moved closer to him. His spicy sweet scent drifted over me, clouding all logical reasoning.

"I love you, Dominique," he said. "And I hate what I have to do to you. I really do."

He cupped my face and brought his lips down on mine. I absorbed every sensation of being with him—his taste, the feel of his tongue in my mouth, his hard body pressed against mine. If only things were different.

But things weren't different.

"You lied to me," I said in a quiet voice, breaking the kiss, but staying close to him and burying my face in the crook of his neck. "You didn't tell me about Fleet being my first love, about Tavion being my uncle."

He pulled me away so he could make eye contact. "I didn't lie about it. I just never mentioned it. Didn't think it was relevant. I'm sorry." His eyes teared. "I wish you'd understand that everything I've ever done has been for you. All of it. Even taking your life will be for you. It's what you wanted."

"Not anymore," I whispered.

"It can't be stopped."

He was right. I knew it. He'd never stop until I was dead. Hugging him tight, I thought of the note I had written to myself. I lifted myself up on my toes and brought my mouth to his ear. "I'm going to kill you first, Farrell."

He kept me close a moment longer before loosening his grip. He combed a strand of hair out of my face. "I hope you can."

He knelt down and scooped up a handful of sand. The grains strained through his fingers until they revealed a white feather in his palm. He handed it to me, studied my face for a moment, and walked toward the calm lake water. With each step, his body disintegrated into wisps of amber and white mist before disappearing all together, blowing away like particles of dust in a gusty wind.

I clutched the white feather, my symbol of hope, and held it to my chest. Breathing in deep and wishing for a different life, I felt the quill start tingling inside my palm. Strangely unafraid, I unfolded my hand and stared at it. The plume started glowing, cycling through hues of red, green, and purple before it pulsed jet black. Ribbons of smoky vapor poured out of it as it floated up and out of reach.

A low tremor shook the ground. The pebbles along the shore started vibrating. Even the bay rippled as if something were churning at the bottom. Moving away from the bank, I noticed gold colored particles all around me. Faint at first, but growing brighter, the pieces hummed and quivered until I realized the flecks were me. I was fading away, too. Just like Farrell.

"What's happening?" I muttered out loud.

The mist around me whirled faster until a blazing flash blinded me. When the brilliance dimmed, I saw a million golden flakes drifting downward, like the sizzle of a dying firework. The choker around my neck fell off. A voice whispered in my ear.

"I hope you can."

My knee jerked, hitting a hard object. Pain shot through my leg. I was confused about where I was, and ready to bolt, until a strong hand grabbed my arm and pulled. "Hey! You're with me!"

I stared at the source of the voice until his identity registered in my brain. "Jake."

"Yeah, Jake."

He started the truck and slowly drove off the ferry. "Geez. What were you dreaming?"

My body bursting into smithereens and the protective choker falling off replayed in my mind. The feather... it must've represented Farrell. If he died, the choker would come off and I'd be normal again. I touched the metal with my fingertips, checking to see if it was still there, and it was.

"Are you going to tell me?"

As we traveled through Galveston, I thought of the prophecy that warned of a change from without. I had to locate my friends, and deep down I knew Trent's grandmother could help. After we were back together, my task was clear. Any doubt about my duty had been erased. "I find my friends. And then I kill Farrell."

Jake gripped the steering wheel. "Damn straight. That asshole is as good as dead."

Chapter Thirteen

~ Trent ~

Matthew and I snaked our way out of the neighborhood, weaving in and out of small streets and flat fields, leaving the police sirens far behind. Right away, I recognized the path back to my church, St. Joseph's, and tensed. "Where are we going?" I called out, worried about getting anywhere near the place where I had been shot.

"My house, not far from St. Joseph's."

Great, I thought to myself, thinking that being near the "crime" scene was a bad idea, but having no other choice.

We rolled down a street with small Victorian homes, not unlike the home where Mother Superior and Sister Mary Catherine lived, and parked inside an open shed behind a small, white wood-paneled home. We scanned the area before hustling into the house.

Wood floors, plain white walls, and almost no furniture — the place almost looked abandoned.

"We don't have a lot," Matthew explained.

Feeling a twinge of pain from my ribs, I slowly lowered myself onto a couch.

"You okay?" Matthew asked.

"Yeah," I said with a groan. "I'll be fine. Just give me a minute. And by the way, I don't have a lot either."

I scanned the area, wondering where Matthew's mom was and if he had any brothers or sisters. Matthew caught on right away. "It's only me and my dad. My mom died two years ago from influenza," he said, making the sign of the cross across his body.

My *abuela* often made the sign of the cross when talking about someone who was dead. She even did it whenever she heard or saw an ambulance, but not me. I was still angry that my parents were taken from me when I was so young, so I refused.

"My mom and dad died in a car crash when I was eight."

Matthew sat beside me, as if sharing the death of a parent put him at ease around his time traveling guest. "So you understand," he said.

I cradled my side. "Yeah, I understand."

Matthew kept his gaze down at the ground, studying his polished uniform shoes. "So, this dame, Dominique. Is she your girl?"

"No. She's not. She's just a good friend."

"Oh," Matthew said, his tone telling me he knew I had other feelings for Dominique.

Compelled to tack on an explanation, I said, "It's a long story."

Before I could say anything else, Matthew's dad burst into the house. He circled the small room, closing the blinds and curtains.

"What's happening?" I asked.

"They're searching the area near the college. After that, they're going to move on to the nearby neighborhoods." He took off his pressed jacket and hat, hanging them on the coat rack in the corner of the room. "It will only be a matter of days before they make it over here."

"I need to get home," I said, the idea of returning to my time suddenly seeming possible. "Right away."

"To the future?" Matthew scoffed, a tone of disbelief lacing his words. He eyed his dad as if searching for validation that the concept was ridiculous. "Dad?"

Roland took a seat in a chair across from me and rubbed the back of his neck. His white undershirt was clean and pressed like the rest of his clothes. "I don't believe in science fiction or time travel, but I do believe there are some things that can't be explained."

I scooted to the edge of my seat, seeing something in Roland's eyes that told me he believed me. "What things?"

He paused for a long while. "Things like a ghost. Maybe even an angel, telling me to help you."

"Long blond hair, big green eyes," I half-whispered.

"Yes," Roland said, stunned. "How did you know?"

"Her name is Abigail, and I've seen her, too. First when you guys carried me out of the church, and then again at the hospital."

"What?" Matthew exclaimed. "Dad, why didn't you tell me?"

Roland rubbed his head. "She came to me in a dream about a week ago, but I didn't think nuthin' of it. Then she came again last night, except I was wide awake. Scared the dickens out of me, she did."

My heart sped up, my body shivered. "What did she say?"

"She told me that you needed me, and for me to stand by you." He studied me with an intense stare. "She glowed with a magical light, and then disappeared right before my eyes."

No one spoke for a while. It was as if Matthew and I were straining to see the image Roland remembered.

"Now what?" Matthew asked.

Roland got up and paced the room. "I don't know. But if the coppers find Trent, he'll fry. We need to think of something. Fast."

Gulping at the idea of being electrocuted for a crime I didn't commit in a time I didn't belong to, I said, "I have an idea." Matthew and Roland came in close. "There's a man named Professor Huxley who used to teach at the college. I think he may have answers."

I thought of how Abigail tricked Huxley into studying her, eventually taking her life so that her energy source could later save Dominique. "I touched the cross," I muttered, staring at my fingertips that activated the cross around Dominique's neck at the red desert where she had almost died. The cross I had seen on my little five-year-old grandfather.

"Kid, ya ain't making sense," Roland said.

"Professor Huxley. He knows about Transhumans," I said. "He's even seen the girl."

"How do you know?" Matthew asked.

Giving them too many details wasn't a good idea, especially since half of it was hard for me to understand, let alone explain. "Roland, Matthew..." I leveled them with a serious yet desperate look. "Please. You have to trust me."

Roland rubbed his creased forehead for a while before nodding. "Okay."

After putting their faith in me, not a whole lot of discussion took place before we formed a plan. They would go out and search for Huxley while I stayed in the house.

Seconds turned into minutes, and minutes turned into hours. Thankful for the time to rest, yet getting nervous as the day became night, I paced the house. My brain imagined they had been caught and questioned. Maybe even beat up and tortured. Expecting the cops to show up any minute and prove me right, I was relieved when the father and son finally came back.

"Did you find him?"

"Yes," Roland said. "He's rented a back room in an upscale house on Caroline Street."

"Great! Let's go."

"Kid, he ain't hardly ever there. I've been told he's been spending a lot of time at the gin mill, pounding the juice."

"Gin mill?"

"You know," Matthew said. "A place that serves hooch." He brought his hand up and pretended to take a swig of beer.

"Are you talking about alcohol?" I asked, wondering what the big deal was, but then remembering about prohibition. "Oh, wait, I get it. It's illegal right now. I forgot."

"It's not illegal where you're from?" Matthew asked, wide eyed.

"Nope. Hasn't been for decades."

"See?" he said to his dad. "I told you that law wouldn't last."

Roland rubbed his chin. "Matthew, that's not what this conversation is about."

"You're right, Dad, sorry."

Roland disappeared into another room and came back with a green duffle bag. "I've got extra clothes and some medical supplies in here." He threw another bag to Matthew. "Load this up with food and water."

Matthew ran to the kitchen, and I heard him opening and closing cabinets and drawers, doing what his father asked.

"Are we going for Huxley?" I asked Roland.

"Yes, but we're going in prepared." Roland and Matthew, suited up in their navy pants and coats, secured their hats on their heads. "If anyone stops us, we say we're on regular patrol. See?" Roland instructed. "And you—" He pointed at me. "You will stay in the bucket until we tell you to come out."

"Bucket?"

"You know, the back of the car," Matthew interpreted. "Where we put the stretcher."

"Oh, gotcha," I replied.

With our bags filled, we got in the hearse-like car that Roland used for an ambulance. With them in the front and me in the back, we set out for Huxley. Huddling in the cold, back cabin, I remembered the pain in my body from the first time I was in here, and fear and doubt crept into my head. What if we got pulled over? What if we didn't find Huxley? Worse, what if we did find him and he couldn't help?

The car creaked to a stop. Panic tingles raced across my skin. I shuffled closer to the open divider between the back of the car and the front, and surveyed the area. The unlit street appeared empty of civilization. There were no houses, only trees. I was about to ask where we were when I finally spotted a small, dark house down the street.

"It's the gin mill," Matthew whispered.

Whoa, so this was what an underground bar looked like in the thirties. Run-down, hidden, and seedy. We watched a few men walking in and out of the house. Some came on bicycles, others had obviously parked their cars out of sight as they disappeared around the corner.

"How will we know which one is Huxley?" I asked.

"I spotted him here earlier, so I can finger him," Roland explained.

After a while, a man came out by himself. Tall and thin, wearing a suit and glasses, he kept in the shadows while he walked down the street. Roland cranked the ignition. "Let's go," he said. He rolled up next to the man. "You Huxley?" he asked through his open window.

Hands in his pockets, the man kept walking and answered in a British accent, "Are you going to arrest me?"

Roland glanced at me and Matthew, the car crawling next to the walking Professor. "No."

"Then bug off."

"Wise guy," Matthew mumbled under his breath.

Desperate for Huxley's help, I craned my neck through the square opening between the front of the car and the back and said hastily, "I'm from the future and Transhumans are real."

The professor stopped. He kept his stare pinned to the ground for a second before eyeing me. "Pardon?"

This was it. I had his full attention and I couldn't blow it. "My name is Trent Avila and I know about the blond girl and what happened to her."

He narrowed his eyes at me and started speed walking. "I have no idea what you are talking about."

I patted Roland's shoulder. "Stay with him," I said, leaning as far over the front seat as I could. The pressure of the seat back made my chest feel on fire, and set my stitches throbbing. "Professor, what happened to her wasn't your fault. She's a Transhuman. She needed her energy in that cross. She tricked you."

Huxley kept walking, ignoring us as if we weren't even there.

A small car, probably his, came into view. My chance at getting his help was slipping away. "I read about it in your journal!" I rushed out.

"Describe it," Roland urged.

"It's brown, and old, and… and… and…" I stuttered, trying to remember exactly what the journal looked like. "It's water stained. And everything is in there. I know all about it."

Huxley slowed to a stop. He brought his hands out of his pockets and placed his trembling fingers on his chin. "I spilled water on it. Yesterday."

"Yes! I know! The pages in the back are hard to read."

He came closer to the car and crouched down, eyeing me. "That's right. The rearmost pages are illegible."

Hollering broke out at the gin mill. Bodies ran from the house. "Jump in, Professor," Roland commanded. "Before we get caught up in whatever ruckus is happening back there."

"Right," he said.

Matthew hopped out, holding the door open for Huxley, and then climbed in the back with me. Hanging my head down in relief, I let out a long breath of air.

"You really think he can help you?" Matthew asked in a hushed tone.

"I hope so."

We drove away from the area, deciding to go to Huxley's since Roland thought his house might be under watch. When we arrived, the professor ushered us to the back of a grand, two-story house with a row of columns out front. It resembled a plantation home.

"I'm in the servants' quarters, over the garage," Huxley said, pointing to the rear of house while we walked up the driveway to another structure.

On the bottom was a two-story garage. Narrow stairs led to a one-room apartment. Inside, piles of paper and scribbled notes covered every available surface, even the floors. I searched for signs that Abigail and my grandfather had been here, but found none. "Is this the place where…" My voice trailed off, not really knowing how to finish my sentence.

Huxley took off his wire-rimmed glasses and wiped them with the edge of his sleeve. He looked tired and worn. "Where I studied the children? No. That was at a place near the Institute. I left there shortly after the…" He put his spectacles back on, unable to finish his train of thought.

Matthew and Roland stayed on their feet, uniformed and looking official. "Please, sit," Huxley said, motioning to a small table and straight-backed chairs.

With my side on fire, I gladly took a seat, but Roland and Matthew declined, preferring to keep watch over me. A gesture I really didn't mind. Huxley eased himself into a chair across from me. He rubbed his short, curly hair. "Would you care to explain yourself?"

"Sure," I said, wiping my sweaty hands on my jeans, thinking the room was warm despite the cold outside. "My name is Trent Avila. I'm from Houston, but in the future. I'm trying to get back to my own time and to my friends. They're in trouble."

He leaned in and studied me with intent eyes. "What kind of trouble?"

"There's a war going on between these Transhumans, and my friend is caught in the middle. She needs my help."

"What do you know of Transhumans?"

He was putting me to the test, using his analytical skills as a scientist and a professor, and I couldn't blame him. Even I wouldn't believe me if I were in his shoes.

"They're like superheroes in the comics," Matthew blurted. I cringed, thinking that hearing an explanation like that only made me sound insane.

"Well, yeah, that," I said in pitiful tone.

"*Make him see*," a voice whispered.

I nearly jumped out of my chair, searching for Abigail, knowing her voice anywhere.

"Trent? Kid? You okay?" Roland asked.

"Of course he is not okay. He's insane. Now please leave my quarters at once," Huxley said, deciding to be an adversary instead of a believer. Apparently, Matthew's comment must've convinced him I didn't know what I was talking about.

My face turned hot as desperation gripped me. I had Huxley back there on the road, but now I'd lost him. My chance at getting home had been dashed with a single swipe.

"*He can see me if you want him too*," Abigail said. A cloudy mist appeared in the corner of the room, her form coming into view as she stepped out from the haze.

I scrambled to my feet, knocking over my rickety chair. "Do you see her?" I asked, awe and surprise heavy in my voice. I pointed to where she stood. "She's right there."

Roland took my arm. "Come on, kid. Let's leave the professor alone."

"*Focus on your light*," Abigail instructed. "*Hurry.*"

Breaking free from Roland's grip, I backed up against the wall and held out my arms, keeping them at bay. "Give me a minute! Please! I'm begging you!"

Matthew darted in front of me, stance wide, arms crossed. Staring down his dad and the professor he said, "Let him have his time." He glanced over his shoulder at me. "Go on."

"And I thought I was crazy," Huxley muttered.

"Hey!" Matthew said. "He knew that stuff about you. So I wouldn't be calling him crazy."

The professor sat back down and rubbed his eyes

under his lenses. "Prove what you say," he said to me. He brought out a pocket watch from the inside of his tweed jacket. "You have two minutes."

"Okay," I said to Abigail. "How do I do this?"

Her glowing image came close, her face peaceful and full of hope. She took my hand and squeezed. Her skin felt warm and soft. Her touch calm and soothing. *"Think of what you want them to see,"* she instructed.

I searched the faces of my audience and saw fear and worry. Knowing I needed to calm them, I relaxed myself and said, "It's okay. Everything is going to be alright." Their shoulders eased. Their worry lines diminished. "If you open your hearts and your minds to the possibility of things we can't explain, you'll see her. You just need to believe."

Roland and Matthew's breathing steadied. Even the professor's demeanor softened.

"Now," Abigail said.

I closed my eyes, willing my aura to shine bright, convinced the others would see her if I could just tap into my potential. A low humming filled my ears. Soft vibrations tickled at my skin. Soothing warmth gathered inside my chest and spread over my body.

"Jesus, Mary, and Joseph," Roland said softly. "It's her."

My eyes opened just in time to see Professor Huxley's watch tumble to the floor. He pushed his chair away from the table and stumbled backward until he collided with the kitchen cabinets. Matthew and Roland huddled together.

Abigail glided toward him. "Don't be afraid, Professor. I was never really alive anyway."

Chapter Fourteen

~ Infiniti ~

At first I hated the idea of traveling in a mom van, but now that we were over a thousand miles into our road trip, I was grateful. Stretching out and taking naps to break the monotony made the journey bearable.

"Finally," Fleet muttered.

Raising my reclined seat, I spotted the "Welcome to Texas" sign. "Yes," I said, relieved that we had made it to the Lone Star State without seeing Farrell again and without being spotted at any truck stops or rest stations. Now, all we needed to do was make it to my house.

Pressing my face against the cool window, I peered up at the clouded-over sky. A wall of dense clouds blocked the hazy sun rays, washing the landscape in different hues of gray. "I wonder what time it is," I said out loud. Neither of us had watches, and the dashboard clock didn't work.

"Around 5:30," Fleet said.

At first, when he said stuff like that, it awed me. Now nothing he said surprised me. I just chalked it up to his Transhuman power thingy. Lowering my seat again, I asked, "How much longer?"

"Five hours. Give or take."

I spent the remainder of the time thinking up different scenarios for when we got to my house. Would my mom be there? The cops? Reporters? Or even Farrell? If we got inside without being busted, would my idea of destroying the Ouija board and cards even work? I knew it was probably a long shot, but if there was any remote possibility of a giant reset button, then I had to try it. Maybe it could even get Trent back.

The closer we got to my house, the more on edge I became... which meant mindless rambling. "Okay, we park at least a street over. We scope out the area, making sure it's clear. When it is, we make our way to my house, staying in the shadows. You can go first, and I'll hang back a little. You can see inside my house through the front windows. If the coast is clear, you can do a bird call. Like this. CA-CAW, CA-CAW, CA-CAW."

Fleet slammed his hand on my leg. "Stop."

"Oh, okay. Sorry," I said with a swallow. "I'm just super nervous."

"I get it," he said. "But I need you to relax."

Filling my lungs with a huge gulp of air, I repeated the word "relax" over and over in my head. "Okay, all better."

"Good," he said. "Now where to?"

When we finally turned into my neighborhood around ten, you would've thought we were entering a weird, paranormal, dead zone. No one was out, not even the occasional dog walker. A hazy fog circled the illuminated light poles. Peering through the tall pines, I caught a glimpse of a huge moon.

My stomach dropped. "Shit, there's a full moon."

Fleet eyed me. "What is it with you regular humans and the full moon?

"Well, it's uh—" I didn't really have a good answer to his question. "It's just bad. And creepy."

When Fleet turned onto my street, I started to say something when he stopped me with a wave. "You really do talk too much."

He was right, and I bit my lip to stop myself. When we passed my house, I ducked a little. Darkness shrouded the two-story brick structure. Not a single light was on inside. "I wonder if she's there. Or maybe she's asleep," I whispered.

Fleet parked in a dark spot, away from the streetlights, and a mere two houses down from mine. He faced me. "We get the board and the cards and then what?"

My heart slammed against my chest. My mouth went dry. "We cut the board into seven pieces and bury it."

"And the cards?"

"We burn them."

Fleet eyed the nearby houses for a minute, tapping the steering wheel. He let out a breath. "Let's go."

Moving quickly, I led him around to the back of the house. I poked my head through the garage door. My mom's car was there as well as the lingering aroma of pot. "Yep, she's home."

At the back door, knowing my mother never locked up, I slowly turned the knob and swung open the door. We shuffled into the kitchen and stood in silence while our eyes adjusted to the lack of light. "She must be in her room," I said softly. "Crashed."

"Good. Now get what we need. I'll wait here."

Tip-toeing across the den, I stole my way up the stairs and to my room. Once safely inside, I flicked on the light. A moan came from my bed. A body turned over underneath my comforter. My mom!

She rubbed her eyes, sat up, and stared at me. "Fin?"

Paralyzed by panic, shivers racing across my skin, it took me a few seconds to answer. "Mom?"

She jumped to her feet, surprise and excitement on her face. "Fin! Is that really you?"

The door to my room flew open, and Fleet came barging through.

"It's okay! It's just my mom!"

Anger shot from my mom's eyes like daggers as she looked from me to him. Her jaw clenched. "You were with a goddamn boy voluntarily?"

Fleet grumbled under his breath, then flicked a blast of vapor at my mom's head. She fell back onto the bed, like a toppled-over mannequin. I pushed him with all my strength. "What the hell!"

He turned on me with fiery eyes. "Listen, I didn't want to come here, but I did anyway. So get your crap and let's go."

Muffled by his harshness, and rubbing my aching wrist that had bent backward when I shoved him, I glanced at my mom. My lip started to quiver. "Is she okay?"

He ran his fingers through his hair. "Yes, she's sleeping."

I tucked her legs under the comforter and positioned the pillow under her head. "Will she remember?" I moved her hair out of her face, feeling sorry for what I was putting her through. I had to be the worst daughter in the world.

"No," he said, his tone now calm and maybe even a remorseful. "She won't. Can we go now?"

Avoiding eye contact with Fleet so he'd know I was pissed, I pulled the Ouija board and my oracle cards from the top shelf of my bookcase.

"Where do we do this?" he asked.

I tried to think of an appropriate spot to murder a Ouija board. Right away I thought of my giant and heavily wooded back yard. Even if my mom woke up, she'd never see us out there. "Backyard."

On the way out, I stopped in the kitchen and started rummaging through drawers. "We need scissors and a lighter."

"No we don't," he informed me. He took the board and the cards, and made his way out to the back.

Bossy.

Crunching through leaves and dried brush because my mom didn't believe in yard work, we reached the back fence and hunkered down. Fleet dropped the board and held up the cards. "Burn these?"

"Yes."

He brushed away a pile of leaves with his boot and created a clear circle of smooth dirt. He set the deck down in the middle. Placing his index finger on the top, he closed his eyes. A spark flickered at his touch. A small trail of smoke rose from the spot. He blew softly and the spark turned into a flame. We watched as the cards Jan had given me, the cards that started Dominique's visions, started to burn.

Feeling the need to say something, I stood and raised my hands up in the air. "Thank you, Jan, for your gift. May it now be a part of the Earth." Held in a trance by the tiny fire, I waited for some magical phenomenon to happen. But nothing did.

Fleet grabbed the board. "Tear this into seven pieces and then bury it?"

"Yes," I murmured.

After breaking the wooden game into the required parts with his bare hands, realizing my scissors would never have done the job, I stared at the letters on the dirt. Sadness over destroying the board that had answered so many questions for me set in, and I wanted to cry.

Of course, Fleet had no clue. Focused on his task, he pointed to a spot next to the flaming cards. A pulsing swirl of vapor came out of his hand with a whoosh. Whisking around in a tight funnel, it hammered into the dirt, creating a medium-sized hole. When it was deep enough, he stopped, dropped the chunks inside, and then covered them up with nearby dirt.

"Done," he said, brushing his hands off. "Let's go."

The smell of ash from the burning cards wafted into the air and stung my eyes as I stared at the makeshift grave for the board. Whimpers escaped my lips, my shoulders shook, and I buried my face in my hands. I had expected a supernatural remedy to make all the crap happening to us and Dominique go away, yet everything stayed the same.

I sunk to my knees. "I'm a failure."

Fleet didn't say anything, but he did join me on the ground. He patted my back. "You tried, Tiny."

Wiping my face, I looked up at him, amazed that he could go from total jerk to completely amazing in a heartbeat. "You know, you're not half bad."

He smiled. "I guess."

"Can I tell you something?" I asked.

"Sure."

Wiping my snotty nose with my sleeve while Fleet waited patiently for me to go on, I confessed. "It's all my fault they found her." I stared at the remains of our ritual, remembering how I had coaxed Dominique into playing the cards and how I had suggested playing the board. "She didn't want to play those cards or the Ouija board, and I convinced her." A puff of wind rustled the leaves and the crisp air cooled my hot cheeks. "I'm to blame. For everything."

He kept quiet. After what felt like an eternity, he said, "Listen, Infiniti, you can blame yourself all damn day, but it was only a matter of time before the Tainted found her." He lifted my chin, making me look at him. "You did not start this. Okay?"

"Okay," I murmured.

He pulled me to my feet and held my shoulders. Strength, hope, and even courage seeped into me with each second I stood in front of him. "But we are going to finish it, Tiny."

I placed my hands on top of his. "Shit yeah, we are."

We wove through my neighborhood and into Trent's. If Trent's grandmother wanted to see Dominique, then she had to have some information on what was going on. I hoped that somehow Dominique had seen the message and would be going there, too. If we were together again, then maybe, just maybe, we could put an end to everything. There had to be a way to save Dominique's last life.

Chapter Fifteen

~ Dominique ~

An awkward silence filled the car as we drove from Galveston to Houston, the kind of quiet that doesn't let you speak even if you wanted to. My mind filled with deaths, the ones I had caused, and the one I had yet to inflict.

Could I really kill Farrell?

"Hey," Jake said, interrupting the drone of the truck's engine, his voice a little hoarse. "There's a mall up there." He cleared out his vocal chords with a cough. "Let's stop and get some clothes."

I had forgotten that I was wearing sweats that were a size too small... and fuzzy socks. "Good idea."

Like a skilled criminal, Jake broke into the closed mall with ease, coming back with a bag of clothes and shoes for both of us. He used his Transhuman powers, and luckily, didn't have to brandish his weapon at any mall cops. Taking turns in the truck, we changed our clothes. Feeling better in clothes that actually fit, I was ready to go when I spotted a few cars still parked in the lot.

"Hey," I said. "Maybe we should ditch this ride and get another in case this one has been reported."

"Okay. You pick."

I eyed the nearby vehicles, feeling like I was a winning contestant on a game show. Because it was late, there were only a few choices available, a van, a black SUV, and two trucks. My attention latched onto the SUV because it had dark tinted windows.

"Is that the one?" Jake said, following my line of sight.

"Yeah."

Breaking into the car was easy for Jake. Once in, we took off for Trent's house. I tried my best to remember the right highways and exits. Getting us turned around a few times, we finally made it to my neighborhood, which was the only way I knew how to get to Trent's since his was right next to mine.

Powerful feelings of regret and remorse sank deep into the pit of my gut, the loss of my dad hitting me harder than ever as we drove down the familiar streets. After everything my dad had done for me, all the sacrifices he had made, he had died trying to save me. Fighting back the surge of tears that threatened to explode out of me, I rested my hand on Jake's as we approached the lake across the street from my old house. "Stop," I whispered, eyeing the two-story, red brick structure where I had lived for only a few months. Such a short amount of time for so much to happen.

"Hey, Dom. It's alright." He took my hand and our fingers intertwined. He squeezed. "I'm here with you now, and everything is going to work out."

Of course I didn't believe him, not after everything, but I nodded anyway. My gaze traveled over to the bench facing the lake. Shrouded in darkness and surrounded by tall pines, that was the place where Trent had found me and took me to his house the first time. It was also where we had the candlelight vigil for Veronica. I pulled my hand away from Jake's. "I need a sec, okay?"

"Sure."

Leaving him in the car, I went to the wooden bench and sat. A full moon shone on the lake, lighting it up with a soft glow. The waterfall in the middle sprayed up and out, forming tiny little ripples on the water. Tears spilled onto my cheeks, and I didn't even wipe them away because I wanted to feel them. Wanted my remorse to flow out of me. I faced my final life not knowing if I would survive, and not really caring anymore.

Footsteps crunched on the nearby gravel jogging path. Looking over my shoulder, wishing it were Trent somehow magically coming to me, I spotted Jake instead. "I can't let you sit here by yourself," he said, joining me. I leaned my head on his shoulder. He held me tight and didn't say a word as my tears flowed quietly.

"Can I tell you something?" I asked him.

"Anything."

Sitting upright, I whispered, "I wished him dead."

"Who? Tavion?"

My shoulders shook from the pain inside me. "My dad." Cool wind whipped all around us, kicking up the dirt and leaves at our feet. I closed my eyes and forced myself to be still. Jake sat quiet too, and I could tell he was waiting for me to explain. "When we moved from Elk Rapids here to Houston, I was so mad, I wished for him to die." I wiped the tears away from my face. "And my wish came true."

"Oh, Dom, listen, that wasn't you." He angled my body toward him and tipped my chin up with his fingers, forcing me to make eye contact. "You didn't do that to him. You have to know that."

"I guess," I said with a shrug.

He rubbed my cold arms. "You need to channel that anger. Avenge your dad. Kill Farrell. It's what he would've wanted."

Jake was right, Dad would want me to do whatever it took to survive, even if that meant killing my former protector and love of lifetimes. I needed to let go of my guilt, no matter how hard. I needed to see this through.

"You ready to go on?"

Scanning the lake, the trees, and the nearby homes, a faint smell of vanilla wafted my way. My heart quickened. I peered at the jogging path. I had seen Jan on that path, the ghost of her anyway. I waited for her to appear, but she didn't. Rising up to my feet, feeling as if that scent prodded me on, I said, "I'm ready."

We arrived at Trent's in less than a minute, parked a few houses away, and watched. The tiny home looked more of a mess than the last time I'd been there. Overgrown grass and weeds had taken over the lawn. Part of the once immaculate picket fence leaned over onto the sidewalk. A strand of unlit Christmas lights hung from the roof, and it was almost March.

"This is it?" Jake asked.

"Yes."

He eyed the shabby house doubtfully. "Well, let's see what she has to say."

Forcing myself to take deep breaths, we made our way to the front door. I knocked, and we waited a second before it swung open. Abuela looked out blankly, her blind eyes clouded over.

"Abuela, hello, it's me Dom—"

"¡Mija! You got my message!"

"Yes, I did." She extended her thick hand to me, and drew me into the house. "I also brought my friend, Jake."

"Jake?" She looked around as if searching for him. I

remembered that she could see auras but was unable to see mine because it was cloaked by my parents. Or at least, now, just my mom. But why couldn't she see Jake's? I thought of his metallic collar under his dark hoodie and wondered if that was why.

"Good evening," Jake said. "I'm Jake, Dominique's friend. It's very nice to meet you."

Abuela's eyes followed the sound of his voice. "Any friend of Dominique's is welcome," she said. *"Mi casa es tu casa.* Now come, *vaminos.* Let's have a bite to eat."

Eat? She wanted a bite to eat? Jake raised his eyebrows at me, and together we followed her to her little yellow kitchen. "Abuela, thank you for offering us food, but don't you think we should…" I paused, trying to figure out what to say.

"Talk?" she asked. "Yes, yes, we will. In a minute."

She motioned for us to sit at the table, and I watched as Jake eyed the many crosses hanging on the wall grouped around a larger-than-life portrait of Jesus in the middle. "Interesting," he whispered to me.

A large pot simmered on the stove. When she lifted the lid, the most sensational aroma of spices filled the air. My mouth watered. My stomach grumbled. "See," she said, giving the contents a stir. "I knew you'd be hungry."

Embarrassed, I covered my stomach with my arms, thinking that having a meal was a really good idea. "I guess so."

"I know I could use a bite," Jake offered with a shrug, giving in to the impromptu dinner break. He stripped off his backpack, set it on one of the empty chairs, and readied himself for a meal.

Abuela spooned the contents of the pot into two bowls, heated up some tortillas on the stove burners, and placed the food in front of us. "This is picadillo. Beef with potatoes. Please eat. I'll be right back."

Jake scooped up a heaping spoonful. "Okay, we eat real quick, then get back to business." Chewing the food as if it were the best thing he'd ever eaten, he let out a groan. "Whoa," he said with his mouth full. "This is freaking awesome."

Taking my own bite, I had to agree with him. The beef hash tasted scrumptious—warm, rich, and spicy. We finished up our bowls in no time. Abuela returned and started tidying up the kitchen. I got up to help, but she made me sit, telling me she preferred cleaning on her own. While she bustled about the kitchen, Jake and I started to grow impatient. His knee bounced under the table while I twisted a strand of hair around my finger.

"Abuela," I said, prompting her to stop wiping her counter. "You said on the news for me to come see you. Can you tell me why?"

She slung her dish towel over her shoulder and joined us at the table. Staring up into blank space, she said, "When they said you and your family died in a car crash, I knew it wasn't true." My blood chilled at her words. "Even my boy, Trenius, knew. He spent days and nights worrying about you. And then, one day, he disappeared into thin air. His *amiga* Infiniti, too." She pointed her thick, crooked finger at me. "I knew it was because of you."

Feeling as if she was accusing me of something and waiting for my rebuttal, I struggled to find the right words. "I-I-I had to leave Houston because some bad people were after me. Trent disappeared because..." I thought of him in this house while Farrell tried to probe his mind and how we had taken him against his will to the Boardman cabin because it didn't work. "We thought he could help me. But the bad people got to him and he's gone now. I'm so sorry."

Her face took on an expression of hope. "He is not gone." She made the sign of the cross, then reached into the pocket of her floral print housecoat. She brought out a worn and yellowed piece of paper. She handed it to me. I leaned toward Jake and unfolded it.

This is Trent. I'm alive and stuck in Houston in 1930. Find Dominique and tell her.

My mouth dropped open. The paper fell out of my hand. Trent had survived the shooting. I knew it.

"He's alive," Abuela whispered. *"Mijo* is alive." Tears of joy sprang to her eyes. She folded her hands on her lap. "And we're staying right here until he finds us."

Chapter Sixteen

~ Trent ~

Professor Huxley stared at Abigail, dumbfounded. He held out a trembling hand, as if trying to ward her off. "What is this? What am I seeing?"

Relieved that everyone could see her so they'd stop thinking me crazy, I answered, "It's Abigail. The girl you studied."

"B-b-but she expired. And then she v-v-vanished."

Roland and Matthew kept quiet, their mouths open, their eyes practically bulging from their sockets.

"I'm here to explain," Abigail said in her young voice, her stare meeting each of ours in turn before landing squarely on Huxley. "I'm here to tell you the truth, Professor."

"What truth?"

She stopped in front of him. "That you didn't do anything wrong. I tricked you into studying me because I needed to pass my energy into the cross around my neck." Her delicate fingers lighted at the top of her white dress. "I planned for the necklace to pass through the generations so Trent would give it to the Marked One and later use the power inside to save her. Which he did."

"Who?" Huxley asked.

"The Marked One, Dominique. She's from the future. She needs to live."

Huxley rubbed his face, his look of shock fading into an expression of relief mixed with curiosity. "I did not kill you?"

"No, you did not."

Huxley let out a sigh of relief. I could almost see the guilt leaving him as his shoulders straightened and his brow relaxed. "So, this Dominique. Why does she need to live?"

"If she dies, the Transhuman race will eventually die, too. If the race expires, it will disrupt the balance of world, the consequences of which have yet to be seen and are largely unknown."

Her precise and formal language seemed odd coming from her small form, yet somehow fitting. She wasn't of our world. In fact, I really didn't understand exactly what she was. All I knew was that she wanted to help me. But what did Dominique have to do with the entire race of Transhumans?

"Do you understand?" She studied the professor's silent form before looking at Roland, Matthew, and then finally me. "Do you all understand?"

"No, not really," I said. "Why will the race die?"

"Farrell will destroy anyone who stands in the way of his task of eliminating the Marked One. There is no changing his path. But what you don't know is that if he's successful, he will continue with the destruction of all the Pures anyway."

"Shit," I muttered, my mind reeling. "Farrell's going to kill everyone no matter what?"

"Yes."

Grasping at the magnitude of her revelation, I

wondered about the Tainted faction of the Transhumans. "What about the dark ones?" I asked her. "The Tainted? What of them?"

"Farrell has already extinguished them. Only a few Pure remain."

"Wait," Matthew interjected. "I thought this Farrell guy was one of the bad ones, one of the Tainted, so does that make him the last one?" Matthew asked, filling in the blanks of the puzzle I was trying to piece together.

"Farrell is warped. He stands alone," Abigail explained. "An abomination. Do you understand now?" Abigail asked.

I nodded, unable to find the words.

"Save the dame, Dominique," Roland answered for all of us. "How?"

Abigail glided my way. Her transparent form started to blur at the edges. The details of her face grew fuzzy and unfocused. "Help Trent get home," she said, fading away like an evening shadow, leaving us speechless.

"Whoa," Matthew said in a hushed tone, taking a seat at the small kitchen table. Dazed. "Did we just see a ghost?"

I rubbed my face. "I don't know what she is, and I can't wrap my head around half of what she said, but she's right. I need to get home and help my friends, and we need to hurry before the cops find me."

"The authorities?" Huxley asked, snapping to. "What do they want with you?"

I spent the next several minutes filling in Huxley on how Dominique, Farrell, Infiniti and I had transported to 1930 and how I had been shot and left behind. He had a million questions, and I did my best to answer each and every one without getting too impatient. But when I heard police sirens in the distance, I started to grow antsy.

"Asking me these questions isn't helping!"

Huxley walked to a small desk. "Questions lead to answers. Answers lead to discovery." He pulled out his brown journal and tore out a sheet of paper.

"That's it! The journal that my friends have in the future! They thought your notes about Abigail could help them. Can I see it?"

He eyed his book and then handed it to me. "I wonder how they acquired it."

"I don't know," I said, flipping through the pages. Half of the book had water damage and smeared text. The other part was okay, but didn't really have anything important that I could see.

"Did my writings aid your friends?"

"Not that I know of."

"Ah," he muttered. "Enough of that, then." He drew a straight line on the sheet. He marked the beginning of the line with an X. "This is you in your proper time." Then he drew a Y at the end of the line. "This is you in this time, right now. The question is" — he circled the open space in the middle — "what transpired that caused you to move from there to here?"

Everyone sat around and stared at the middle section of the line. "Well," I said, "my friends and I were in Michigan outside by a fire. It was during the day and we were talking, when a group of Tainted attacked us."

"The bad guys that are now dead," Matthew said, making sure he was getting his facts straight.

"Yes."

My thoughts went to that icy day. I remembered the look of fear in Dominique's eyes. Could smell the fire in the air from the volley of energy blasts. "Farrell had diverted his energy source to protect Dominique, so he couldn't transport us out of there. He asked me to do it, saying I had the power. He instructed us to hold hands and told me to think of a safe place. I did what he asked, thinking of my church, St. Joseph's. We made it there, but I didn't mean for us to time travel."

"So if your colleague, this Farrell, said you have the power, then you must still have it."

My head hung low. "That's just it, I don't."

"How do you know?" the professor asked.

"Because I've tried."

Huxley took the pencil to paper and started drawing a circle. "Energy," he mumbled as he continued the circular motion. "Connection." The marks on the paper grew darker with each stroke. "Together." Pressing with frantic speed, the tip broke. "I have it!"

"What?" I asked, perked up and hopeful that his scientific mind had the solution on how to get me back home.

"You all held hands. Your energy needed theirs."

"You mean my energy won't work without them?"

"Precisely."

Matthew, Roland, and I stared at Huxley, clearly unable to understand what he meant by my energy needing theirs. Huxley put on a professorial look and said, "Energy is the ability to do work. Work is moving something against a force, like gravity." He eyed us for a second. "Let me explain it this way. There's a novel I've read. It is outside my scope of expertise, and filled with notions that some call ludicrous. It's called *The Time Machine*."

"Yeah, by H.G. Wells," I said.

"You know it?" the professor asked, impressed with my knowledge.

"Sure. I mean, I've seen the movie. Not the whole thing, but I know the gist of it."

Professor Huxley stared at me. "A movie?" Then he shook his head, as if to get back on track. "In the tale, the professor builds himself a time machine equipped with lights and dials and other operational gadgets."

"Okay, I get it. But guess what, I didn't have a fancy car or machine or anything like that."

He pointed at me. "*You* are the machine. Your friends are your lights and dials."

Desperate, feeling like we were going nowhere and I was stuck here forever, where I would probably be arrested and sentenced to the death penalty, I blurted, "But they're not here!"

Huxley paced the room. Wrapped up in his own thoughts, he grabbed a fresh pencil from his desk and started having a full on conversation with himself. "We get all of you in the same location. The exact same place. Once you are positioned, you hold hands, as it were, and concentrate on getting back together."

"Hold hands? Someone from this time with someone from the future? Are you nuts?" Roland asked the professor.

"I mean it in the metaphysical sense. And yes, good sir, I believe I may be slightly nuts." He went back to his paper and drew a square around the line. He put an X in middle, then looked at me. "We need a place."

Ready to believe in anything, and going along with Huxley's theory because I had nothing else, I thought of places that existed both in the 1930s and in the future during my time. Even though I didn't want to go back there, I knew the perfect structure right away. "St. Joseph's Catholic Church."

Huxley tapped his pencil on the table. "Your entry point will be your exit point. Brilliant. Now all we need to do is tell them where to meet you."

"Is that all?" Matthew scoffed.

I thought of scribbling that note for Dominique and giving it to my great-grandmother, Carmen. Abigail had said she had received the message. And then I spotted Huxley's leather journal. I swooped it up and held it. "They have this journal!"

"And?" Huxley said to me, excited to see where my thoughts were taking me.

"We leave them a note in it—"

"And they'll get it!" Matthew exclaimed, finishing my sentence for me, and totally buying into my sci-fi logic.

"Yeah," I said with a smile. "Why not? It's worth a shot, anyway. Right?"

I took the pencil and wrote, "*This is Trent. I'm alive, and I'm trying to get home. Go to St. Joseph's, at the spot where we were standing when I got shot. If you concentrate on me, I think I can transport back. Please hurry. I'll be waiting.*"

Huxley tucked the journal into his coat pocket. "Let's get on, then."

Piling into Roland's ambulance, we headed for the church. Anxious and on edge, we didn't talk at all. When we arrived at St. Joseph's, we found the front entrance manned by a lone police officer.

"Great. Now what?" I asked.

Roland parked out of sight and thrummed the steering wheel. "I'll go up there and tell the copper that I'm on patrol, helping the chief with his search. I'll lead him away from the door. You three go in and do what you need to do."

"Sounds like a solid plan," Huxley said. "And by the way, if this works, and we witness a time travel event, no one can mention it. Ever. Understood?"

"Ever?" Matthew asked.

"Ever," Huxley said again with force behind each syllable. "Unless you *want* to spend the rest of your days in an insane asylum. I assure you it is a most unpleasant place."

"Yeah, you're right," Matthew said. "No one would ever believe it anyway."

"So we agree to keep this between us?" Huxley asked.

Roland stuck his hand out, and Matthew placed his on top. Like a team in a huddle before a big game, I added mine next, and Huxley followed. "Agreed," we all said.

Roland casually approached the entrance, started talking to the cop, and then the two of them sauntered down the street, joking and laughing. Matthew, Huxley, and I waited until they were out of sight before dashing for the door. Once inside, we caught our breath, and studied the empty space. Streaks of light from the full moon outside beamed through the stained glass windows. A spotlight at the front of the church illuminated the altar and the crucified form of Jesus. I shivered as I studied the deadly representation. Fear filtered through me. I remembered the image of the *curandera's* death card.

"You okay?" Matthew asked.

"Yeah," I said, forcing myself to get it together. "I'm fine. Let's go to the front. That's where I was when I was with my friends."

Even though we were alone, we did our best to keep quiet as we made our way to the front of the church. I stood at the exact spot where I had been shot. Studying the floor, I halfway expected to see traces of my blood, but the marble was spotless. I imagined the nuns on all fours scrubbing with large buckets of soap and water.

"This place gives me the creeps," Matthew said,

eyeing the walls as if a scary monster would jump out at any minute.

"Me too," I said, feeling sad that a place I used to love and consider safe now evoked an entirely new feeling for me.

"Is this where it happened?" Huxley asked me. "Where you were shot and left behind?"

"Yes."

"All right," Huxley said, taking out his pocket watch. "You stay here. This young man, Matthew, and I will take a seat and observe."

Huxley and Matthew shifted over to the front pew and sat. Matthew's knee bounced. Huxley pulled out his journal and started scribbling notes. Suddenly I felt like a giant science experiment, and I hated it. "Do you have to do that?"

Huxley folded the journal and put it away. "My apologies. Force of habit."

Waiting for something to happen, my pulse raced with anticipation. The pain in my chest started to burn. I nervously shoved my hands in my jean pockets and rocked back and forth on the balls of my feet. I tried to believe my friends had received my message, but it was hard.

"I knew you'd be back," a deep voice sneered.

Spinning around on my heels, I saw Mother Superior emerge from the shadows. She held a large, wooden crucifix and pointed it at me. "You are the devil, son."

Matthew and Huxley sprang to their feet. I waved them away, not wanting them to get hurt by the lunatic Mother. "No-no-no," I stammered, trying to find an adequate response for the nun. "You've got it all wrong."

The Veronica look-alike nun came out of the shadows next, and stood beside Mother Superior. She pointed her long pistol at me, and then waved it at my companions. "Stay back," she warned.

"Young lady!" Huxley called out. "Put that down this instant!"

"You all are of the devil," Mother Superior declared, spit flying out of her mouth. "Spawns from hell. And you must be dealt with accordingly." Her face was stone cold, her stare icy and deadly.

Two more nuns stepped out of the darkness. They carried ropes and candles and what looked like jugs of holy water. Was this some sort of exorcism ambush? My heart sank, my hopes of getting home dashed by these overzealous and superstitious nuns. And then, I began to wonder, since nothing ever went my way, did I need to stay here in 1930? Maybe I needed to die in this time. Maybe that card was destined to come true no matter what.

"*Not today*," Abigail's voice whispered at my ear.

Scrambling for any kind of plan, I held my arms out. If they thought I was the devil, why not play the part? "Stop!" I called out, waving my arms frantically. "Or I will unleash my... wicked power and..." I searched my brain for a religious term. "Smite you with my evil force!"

The nuns froze with fear. Mother Superior almost dropped her talisman. Catching them off guard, Matthew snuck up behind the group and snatched the pistol away. He turned it on the pack and hollered to me, "Do it! Now!"

"Yes," the professor added. "Call your people."

The sisters must've thought Matthew and Huxley were talking about me calling out to demons or devils or something because the black-robed women cringed away from me in fright. Almost down on her knees, Mother Superior raised the crucifix high up in the air. Her look of defiance was replaced with terror.

Knowing this was it, my last chance to get home, I closed my eyes. I focused on my friends in the future. As I willed my aura to extend out of me like a bridge between times, my face began to tingle. My skin shivered with warmth. My entire body felt so adrenaline-pumped I thought I could take off like a rocket and soar through the skies.

"God help us!" Mother Superior wailed.

Cracking my eyelids open, I saw a swirl of blue vapor pouring from my body. It gathered around the floor like a majestic whirlpool. It was working! I was doing it! If what Huxley said about me needing my friends' energy to activate mine was true, then my friends in the future had to be in my very spot.

Come on, I said to myself. *Show yourselves.*

Chapter Seventeen

~ Infiniti ~

Staring at Trent's house, I thought of the last time I'd been here. Dominique had surprised me at the front door. I remembered being so relieved to see her alive after thinking her dead in a car crash, only to have my excitement turned to horror when I saw Farrell mind probing Trent's limp body with his energy stream. That was also the first time I had met Fleet.

"You do the talking, Tiny," Fleet said, giving the door two quick knocks, jarring me from my memory. "If Dominique is in there, don't mention her mom. Or Colleen. Got it? She doesn't need that right now."

"Yeah, okay," I said, shifting in my boots, pulling at my knuckles. "No word about her mom."

The door swung open, and Abuela smiled. Her cloudy eyes landed on me. *"Mija*, Infiniti, I was hoping you'd come." Abuela had always been able to "see" my aura. At first it freaked me out, but after being friends with Trent for a while, I started getting used to it. Her gaze drifted over to Fleet. "Who's your friend?"

"His name is Fleet. He's helping me."

"Ah," Abuela said. "Any friend of Infiniti's is welcome. Please, come in."

Fleet raised an eyebrow at me, no doubt wondering why Trent's grandmother was being so calm. I thought the same thing, especially since there was a nationwide manhunt going on for me and her grandson.

The tiny old lady led us through the den and into the kitchen where delicious smells lingered in the air. The table had been cleaned, but remnants of a recent meal were piled in the sink.

"It's safe," Abuela said out loud. "You can come out."

A door on the other side of the yellow refrigerator swung open. Out came Dominique and a tall, skinny guy. My mouth hung open, my eyes bulged. *What the*?

"Infiniti!" Dominique darted over to me and squeezed me tight. "I thought I'd never see you again!"

I held her as hard as I could, muted by the massive lump that had formed in my throat. When my shock started fading, I pushed her to arm's length and shook her. "Don't you ever leave me like that again! Okay?"

"Okay," Dominique answered, her eyes teary and tired. "I won't."

Dominique's gaze left mine and landed on Fleet. "Hey," she said, the look on her face telling me she must've figured out that she and Fleet had been a thing in her first life. "It's good to see you."

"Yeah, you too," Fleet said. After a road trip with him I picked up on the hurt in his words right away. I wondered if Dominique could too.

Dominique looked past us, as if waiting for someone else to enter the kitchen. "Where's my mom?"

"She went out on her own to look for clues," Fleet said, the lie coming quickly and easily. "She said she'd hook up with us later."

"I'm Jake," Dominique's tall companion said, sticking his hand out to me for a shake.

Fleet held me back, grabbed Jake's hand, and did a ninja move on him, pulling his arm around and slamming him into the wall. "Where the hell have you been?" Fleet asked, the veins in his neck popping out with rage. "Huh?"

"¡Ay, no!" Abuela called out. "No fight!"

"Fleet!" Dominique hollered. "Stop!"

Fleet smooshed Jake's face harder into the wall. One of the crosses over his head toppled over and crashed to the floor. "You piece of shit. Talk now before I kill you dead right here."

"I ditched, I know! I'm sorry! But I'm back! And I want to help! Look at Dominique's neck. That choker I made is keeping her safe!"

Fleet let Jake go and peered at Dominique. She lowered her shirt collar, exposing a metal choker. "It's true," she said. "It's the only way I was able to get away from you all. It's also the only way I can keep hidden from Farrell."

Jake lowered his hoodie and showed us his. "See? I have one, too." He pointed to a black backpack in the corner of the kitchen, his finger shaking. "I have more."

Panic raced through my veins as I remembered my conversation with Farrell back on the highway in Michigan. "Oh my God, we made a deal with Farrell. Shit, shit, shit. We told him we'd let him know when we found you. It was the only way to keep him from killing us."

"The collars," Jake blurted, grabbing his pack. "Put them on. Now."

I started running in place, nervous and freaked out that Farrell would blast into the kitchen like a murderous thunderbolt and kill us all. "Hurry!" I called out to Jake.

Jake fumbled with the zipper for a few seconds, then shoved the collars at me and Fleet. Of course, being a bad ass who didn't take orders from anyone, Fleet hesitated. But not me. I wrapped the collar around my neck, and it snapped into place. Tiny spines embedded in my skin. Pain shot through me. I yelped, ready to claw the thing off.

"Relax," Dominique said, taking my hands. "The collar is positioning itself. That digging feeling will go away in a minute. Okay?"

Forcing myself to chill, I closed my eyes and slowed my breathing. The probing faded. The pain dissipated. "Okay," I said, letting out a breath. "That's better." I glanced at Fleet. "Now you. And hurry before your possessed brother finds us." Fleet eyed the instrument suspiciously. "Don't be a baby," I added.

He squinted at me, murmured something about me being a pain in his ass, and then latched the metal into place. If the collar bored into his skin, or hurt him at all, he gave no indication.

"Your color, all of you," Abuela said, dumbfounded. "*¡Ha desaparecido!* It's gone!"

"Color?" Jake asked.

"Our auras," Dominique explained. "She can see them, so can Trent."

"Oh." Jake relaxed and slunk down onto a kitchen chair. "Yes," Jake said. "This device, which I call a veil, cloaks us. When she says color she must be referring to our energy signature." He tapped his neckware. "With these on we're hidden and safe."

"Yeah, but for how long?" I added, still scared of Farrell finding us and killing us dead.

"Long enough to do what needs to be done," Dominique stated, her words sure, her face resolute.

"Which is?" Fleet asked.

"Find Trent so we can all be together again and

then" — she paused — "kill Farrell." Dominique picked up a piece of paper from the table. She handed it to me. Fleet stood behind my shoulder and together we read the note.

This is Trent. I'm alive and stuck in Houston in 1930. Find Dominique and tell her.

"What the heck?" I looked from the note, to Dominique, to Fleet, and then back to the note. "Is this for real?"

"Yes," Dominique said. "He's alive, Infiniti. Really alive."

The image of Trent being shot in the thirties by that psycho Veronica look-alike nun replayed in mind. "We have to get him," I said.

"From the past? How?" Jake asked.

Dominique paced the room, Fleet leaned against the kitchen counter, and I sat at the table. "How," I repeated. "How, how, how."

"Abuela," Dominique said, lifting the note. "Where did this come from?"

"I was sifting through an old shoe box and found it. I knew it was important from the way it felt in my hand. So I took it to my friend at church, and she told me what it said."

"Were there any other notes in there?" Fleet asked. "Anything else that can help us find Trent?"

"No," she answered, her expression of hope slightly dashed. "That was the only one."

"A note from the past," Jake said. "Very clever."

"Yeah," I said. "Trent's super smart."

"He is," Dominique agreed. "If he left us one message, I'm sure he left us another. But where?"

Silence spread through the small kitchen. Worry and fear for Trent mounted inside me. Maybe there was no second message in Abuela's box because something bad had happened to Trent after all, something *after* he had written that note. A hard shudder passed through my body. An uneasy feeling invaded me. Dominique sat next to me and put her arm around me.

"I'm so afraid for him," I said to her in a whisper.

"Me too, Infiniti. Me, too."

"Hey," Fleet said. "What about this?" He pulled Professor Huxley's journal from his jacket pocket. "Maybe something in here can help us."

Dominique took the book. "This journal couldn't help me remove my mark, but maybe that's not why Abigail gave it to me." She leafed through the pages. "Maybe this book can help us find Trent. It was written back in the 1930s after all, and that's where Trent is." Scanning the text, she stopped toward the end of the journal. Her eyes grew wide.

"What is it?" I asked.

She read out loud, *"This is Trent. I'm alive, and I'm trying to get home. Go to St. Joseph's, at the spot where we were standing when I got shot. If you concentrate on me, I think I can transport back. Please hurry. I'll be waiting."*

"Hell to the yeah," I said. "Let's get our friend."

We piled into the mom van and made our way to Trent's church. Fleet and I sat in front. Dominique and Jake took the back. No one spoke the whole way there, as if we were on our way to a funeral, and maybe we were. Thoughts of death and doom plagued me. Bouncing my knee and shifting in my seat, I tried to distract myself with thoughts of parties and fun, but nothing worked.

Fleet gave me a sideways look. "You okay, Tiny?"

"Yeah." I started to chew my nails, wishing I had some gum. "I'm fine."

"It's going to be okay," Dominique offered, resting her hand on my shoulder.

Even though I wanted to believe her, my usual optimism had vanished. A sinking feeling of dread had taken over me, and I couldn't shake it. Trying to fake my way into a better mindset, I said, "I know."

We parked down the street from the church. The area was dark and quiet, except for the glow of the full moon that shone down on the religious structure like a spotlight. I eyed the nearby house that back in the thirties belonged to the nuns. It looked exactly the same—plain and old-fashioned, with one main exception. It clearly wasn't a nunnery anymore. A red wagon and little pink bike lay on the grass by the front door.

"I wonder if they know crazy nuns used to live there," Dominique said to me.

I shivered. "I know I wouldn't want to know."

Jake slung his backpack over his shoulder, and the four of us crept to the main entrance. Fleet turned the knob and found it locked. A stream of light pulsed from his hand, and the door swung open with a click. Once inside, we took stock of the area for a few seconds before making our way to the spot at the front where Trent had been shot.

"This is the place?" Jake asked.

"Yeah," Dominique and I said simultaneously. "This is it."

Jake set his backpack on the floor by his feet. Fleet directed everyone to hold hands. When I moved into place, a surge of doubt entered my mind. I always paid attention to my instincts, without fail, but should I this time? Trent needed us to get him home. Delay would only make things worse. *Right?*

"Infiniti," Dominique whispered. "What is it?"

"I don't know," I whispered to her. She shot me a confused look, but didn't press it, and I knew why. We were here. Together. And Trent was left for dead in the past. We had to follow through with our plan to rescue him. No matter what.

Standing together, hands clasped, Fleet said, "Jake and I will send out our energy. If Trent is here, even in a different time, we should be able to reach him."

The cold marble floor chilled my petite frame. Moonlight streamed through the stained glass windows, casting long shadows through the sanctuary. Waves of fear, doubt, and uneasiness swept through me. Glancing at Dominique and seeing the color drained from her face, I knew she felt the same way.

I was anxious for the light show from Fleet and Jake to start so we could rescue Trent and ditch the spooky cathedral, and it seemed forever before the sparks finally started emitting from their hands. Slow at first, the sizzles quickened to rapid fire bursts. Fleet's gray vapor poured out of his fingers and gathered at our feet. Jake's oozed out too. Pale yellow and so light you could hardly see it, it mixed with Fleet's, hissing and crackling with each touch. Strengthening in intensity and speed, their energy swirled around the floor like a hurricane formation, and we were the eye. The quicker it whirled, the larger it became until it enveloped the entire floor of the church.

Overcome with awe at the supernatural phenomenon around us, I spied another color breaking through. Soft white at first, the new color turned bright blue, streaking through the air like a lightning storm of ocean-colored intensity. I knew it was Trent. A hazy form began to take shape in the middle of our ring. A stream of blue power shot out of the body like a beacon until the figure fully formed and Trent came into view. His stare met mine, then darted to Dominique. Instead of looking relieved, his face carried an expression of panic. He turned his head. Following his gaze, I saw a group of nuns by the altar, a tall, commanding one in the front that I recognized right away — Holy Mother Freakin' Superior.

Her brow furrowed. Her lip curled. Anger filled her eyes. She started coming for us with a massive crucifix in hand like a crazed demon hunter, when another person sprang into view, a cute guy dressed like a solider with a row of shiny gold buttons down his coat. Another person appeared, a nerdy man with glasses. They blockaded the nun's path, hollering at Trent to get out of there.

"We have to get him!" Dominique yelled.

Fleet quickly assessed the situation. "Do it!"

Dominique broke the circle. She lunged for Trent. At the same time, the blond Veronica-looking nun jumped on the sailor guy's back. They grappled at something in his clutches. The man in glasses joined the skirmish.

"I got him!" Dominique called out.

"Power down!" Fleet ordered.

Everyone dropped hands. The energized hues from Fleet, Jake, and Trent grew dim. Their multi-colored particle blasting started to lose steam. Jake collapsed to his knees with exhaustion, while I kept my eye on the 1930s melee happening just a few feet away from us.

Why aren't they disappearing?

The two guys and the nuns kept at it with the fighting and the hollering. Finally, the space around them grew fuzzy and their forms started blending in with the shadows. It was as if they were being sucked back into their own time where they belonged, like the dimming of an old movie. Relieved, I turned to check on Trent. A pop snapped through the air. Something slammed against my body. I tumbled over in a heap of shocked confusion. My ears rang. My chest burned. Dominique and Trent huddled over me, and a white light formed behind them.

"Hello, my dear." It was Jan, my neighbor from across the street who had given me the oracle cards. Her face looked radiant. Her body glowed with a peaceful shimmer. She came up behind my friends and stretched her hand between them. She stroked my cheek, her touch as soft as cotton, her presence as soothing as a lullaby.

"Hey," I answered with a smile, the word coming out of my mouth nice and slow, lingering for a moment on my tongue. Then I remembered she was supposed to be dead, killed in a plane crash. Yet here she was, talking to me and touching me. My heart skipped with joy. "What are you doing here?"

"I'm here to take you to the other side."

Chapter Eighteen

~ Dominique ~

"No-no-no-no," I pleaded. An icy chill spread across my body. Disbelief and fear grappled my gut. I didn't even know what had happened. Couldn't process the reality before me. Infiniti couldn't have been shot. Not her. Not my best friend.

"Infiniti! Hey!" I begged, cradling her head. "Don't do this to me." Her eyes had a faraway look, and she started mumbling, as if talking to someone right behind me. "Stay with me. Don't leave. Please, please, please, Infiniti."

Looking over my shoulder, I caught the fading image of the group of black robed women. Mother Superior still held her crucifix. The Veronica-look-alike nun kept her pistol at the ready. Consumed with fiery rage, I scrambled to my feet, grabbed the gun from the back of Jake's jeans, and started firing at the sisters.

Pop, pop, pop, pop.

When the chamber emptied, I found myself in the spot where the nuns had been, yet they were gone. Transported back to the past where they belonged. All that was left was me, Trent, Fleet, Jake, and a wounded Infiniti.

Or is she dying?

I rushed back to her. Blood saturated her shirt, oozing all over the fabric and spreading like a liquid wildfire. The color drained from her face. "I'm ready," she said, not looking at any of us huddled around her, but still peering into the distance. Was she talking to an angel? Maybe Abigail or Jan? I had seen them both when I had almost died, so maybe this was the same thing. "Wait a sec," Infiniti said to the invisible entity, taking a deep breath between each word.

She moved her attention to me and the others. "Hey," she said with a weak smile. "Don't be sad. This is only my first life. I'll be back. Tell my mom I—"

Her lips stopped moving. Her eyes froze. Her head fell to the side.

I stared at Infiniti's lifeless form, waiting for her to wake up, my mind struggling to comprehend what had just happened. "Infiniti," I whispered. Tears gushed out of me, strangling my vocal chords, preventing me from saying her name again. I scooped her up and held her to me, rocking back and forth. The weight of losing her crushed my very heart and soul into oblivion, and I wanted to die too.

Staring into the space where she had been looking, I yelled, "Why didn't you save her! You could've saved her!"

Trent edged closer. Sobs escaped his lips. He wrapped his arms around me, and we held Infiniti together, bound by sorrow over the loss of our friend, neither one of us wanting to let go, the word "no" coming out of my mouth over and over.

A hand lighted on my shoulder. "Dominique," a voice said. Peering through my tear-filled eyes, I saw Fleet crouched down beside me. His eyes were red, his face pained. "We need to go."

"I can't do it anymore," I whispered to him. "I can't."

"She'd want you to," he said. He wiped his face, gazed up at the ceiling, then back at Infiniti before meeting my eyes again. "She'd be pissed if you didn't."

Fleet was right. I knew she'd be mad as hell if I gave up, and so would my dad. Deep down I didn't want to surrender. But how could I recover from this? Was it even possible? I had lost my best friend.

"Um, guys," Jake said, timidly holding one of the metal collars. "Trent needs to put this on before Farrell finds us."

Trent and Fleet climbed to their feet. Arguing broke out about the collar, about leaving, and about Farrell coming to kill us all, but I didn't care. Nothing mattered anymore. My friend had just died in my arms.

"I'm so sorry," I whispered to her. My body shook, my brain still working to process what had happened. "Infiniti," I said again, "I'm so sorry."

Still holding her close, I willed her to hear me, prayed for a miracle, waited for her to come back to life and take a deep breath. "Please, come back." I stroked her cheek, her red blood smearing from my hand across her white skin. "You have to come back."

Trent's face came back into view. His lips moved, but I couldn't hear him over my pain, couldn't understand his words through my grief. He gently shook my shoulders. "The cops are coming. We have to go," he said. "Now."

Trent's warning moved slowly through me. His directive fell flat on my ears. Even though I knew I needed to do as he said, knew we needed to go, I didn't want to. The thought of causing Infiniti's death and then leaving her alone ripped me apart.

"It's okay," he said.

"It will never be okay," I muttered.

Staring at her, ready to stay in this church and face the cops or Farrell or whatever might come, I watched Fleet kneel down. With a tear-streaked face, he closed Infiniti's eyes and smoothed her wavy hair. Getting back up, he held his hand out for me. "She'd want you to go on."

My body shaking with sorrow, I leaned over and kissed Infiniti's cold cheek. "Good-bye, Infiniti."

Piling back into the van, having saved one friend but losing another, we headed out of town. Trent agreed it'd be best not to contact his grandmother until everything was behind us, but was that even possible? Would any part of this saga ever really be behind us?

Empty. Lost. Destroyed. I was beginning to think my final death was inevitable, and those connected to me were destined to die, too. Staring out the window, gazing up at the lonely full moon and the almost invisible stars, I said to myself, *I'm sorry.*

Chapter Nineteen

~ *Trent* ~

"Where to?" Fleet asked, driving out of downtown Houston and heading toward a cluster of intersecting highways. I eyed Dominique in the back seat next to Jake to see if she had any suggestions, but I didn't think she had even heard Fleet. She leaned against the car window, her arms tight around her waist, her gaze set on the sky above.

Reading the exit signs, Fleet asked, "North toward Dallas or South toward Galveston?"

"Galveston," Dominique said softly. "That's where we'll finish this. Once and for all."

Settling in for an hour-long ride, my wound at my side sore and stinging from the explosive scene back at the church, my mind drifted to Roland, Matthew, and Professor Huxley. Were they okay? Then I wondered about everything that had happened here in the present while I was with them. I eyed Fleet. "What happened to you and the others after I got shot and left behind?"

Talking low, Fleet filled me in, telling me how Dominique's dad had been mind controlled and used by Colleen, how Colleen escaped but Mr. Wells had been killed. He then told me how Dominique had ditched him,

Infiniti, and her mom. He paused at the mention of Dominique's mom, running a finger across his neck. Then he put his index finger on his lips and jerked his head toward the back seat, letting me know that Dominique had no idea about her mother's death.

Taking another peak at the back seat, I saw that Jake had scooted over to her. Her head rested on his shoulder. I gave them their privacy, overcome with sadness at everything that had happened so far, still shocked about Infiniti. I wondered how much more Dominique could take and I was insanely jealous of Jake's closeness to the woman who had my heart.

"What about you?" Fleet asked. "What happened in 1930?"

My story didn't matter anywhere near as much as Dominique's, and it was the last thing I wanted to talk about, so I kept it short. "I found Huxley and he suggested my power would activate if we were in the same place."

"That's it?"

I could've told him about the hospital, the crazed nuns, my ancestors, and my ambulance driver rescuers, but right then none of that seemed important. "Yeah, that's pretty much it."

Driving out of Houston, past a trail of tiny towns, and finally through Galveston itself, we stopped when the highway ended and faced the expansive Gulf of Mexico.

Jake sat up in his seat. "To the left is the ferry to Bolivar Island and we definitely don't want to go that way."

"Why not?" I asked him.

"Dominique and I were there earlier, and there's a possibility we're wanted for breaking and entering and car theft."

"Great," Fleet muttered, turning to the right and driving parallel to the ocean. "Anything else we need to know, Jake?"

The name rolled off his tongue like a bad word, and for once I sided with Fleet on thinking something was up with our new companion.

"Nope, there's nothing else."

We traveled mostly alone on the two-lane highway. Except for a few cars here and there, it felt like we were the only ones on the road. After a while, Fleet slowed down, his gaze focused on a lone house that faced the water. Completely dark with no sign of life or vehicles, it looked abandoned.

"This should do," Fleet announced, cutting the headlights and turning down a gravel driveway.

He parked on the other side of the house, out of view from the road, and we quickly made our way up into the one-story, stilted, beach home. Sparsely furnished and covered in a film of dust, but equipped with the necessities like central air and heat and a partially stocked pantry and fridge, we could hole up here as long as we needed. Or, at least, until Dominique recovered from her grief.

"Nobody bother me," she said, dragging her body into one of the rooms and shutting herself away from us.

After she disappeared, Fleet muttered something about needing fresh air. He went outside, leaving me and Jake alone in the den. I eased myself onto a leather couch, cradling my side and muffling a groan.

"Are you hurt?" Jake asked.

"I'm fine," I said, ignoring the ache and studying the stranger who had joined our cause. "So who are you anyway? And why does Fleet hate you?"

Jake rubbed his face, stretched out his legs, and stared

up at the ceiling. "I'm Dominique's best friend from first life. We grew up together, did everything together, but when Fleet entered the picture, we slowly grew apart."

"Fleet? Or do you mean Farrell?"

"No, Fleet, her boyfriend at the time. They were even engaged, or betrothed as we called it back then. "

I sat up, ignoring the sharp stab at my side. "Fleet?"

"Yeah." He jerked his thumb in the direction of the door that led out to the porch. "That guy. Though I have learned that at some point Dominique and Farrell became a thing."

Silenced by the revelation, I reclined back to a less painful position, suddenly feeling sorry for Fleet and understanding why he had been such a jerk. "What else?"

"Dominique's dad used to be Tainted, but he switched sides when he fell in love with Caris."

"Her dad? Are you sure?"

"Yes. You can even ask Fleet if you don't believe me. But that's not even the worst part," he said.

"There's more?"

Jake didn't say anything for a few seconds, as if trying to find the right words. "Dominique's dad and Tavion were brothers."

Like a punch to the gut, I forgot to breath. My gut tensed. "Brothers?"

"Yes. Tavion was so enraged when Stone deserted their kind that he marked Dominique for death." He made a swooping motion with his arms. "That's what this whole thing is about."

My mind raced, and I could hardly believe what Jake had said. Then I thought of Farrell and Fleet, brothers on opposite sides of a supernatural war just like Dominique's dad and uncle. Talk about family drama. But it still didn't explain why Fleet despised Jake.

"Going back to the hatred between you and Fleet, it was all because you and Dominique were best friends?"

"That, and I left the cause." Jake let out a sigh. "I was supposed to be part of her defense team, but I didn't follow through."

Some best friend, I thought, immediately thinking him a coward for not standing with Dominique. Who would do that?

As if reading my mind, Jake added, "I'm a dick, I know. But things got complicated, and I lost my way."

The door swung open, and in came Fleet followed by a gust of cool air. The house shuddered as the furnace kicked on and warmth jetted out from the vents. Fleet took a seat across from me and Jake, legs wide, brow stitched together. If he were any angrier, he'd be on fire.

"Dominique's right, we need to finish this. No more running. No more hiding. If we die. If we live. No matter the outcome. We do whatever the hell we need to do to end this war." He formed a fist, his knuckles white, the veins popping out of his hand. "For Infiniti. You got me?"

Like a warrior being pumped for battle, courage raced through my veins and I was ready to charge into whatever lay before me to protect Dominique and avenge Infiniti. "I'm in," I said. "All the way. For Infiniti."

Fleet glared at Jake. "And you?"

"I wouldn't be here if I wasn't in."

Fleet glanced at the door of the room where Dominique had retreated. "We'll give her whatever time she needs, but when she comes out, we'll have a plan. So let's figure it out."

"We need to kill Farrell," Jake said without hesitation. "It's the only way."

I thought of what Abigail had told me, and agreed

with Jake. "Farrell will either kill us to get to her, or kill us after her."

"What?" Fleet asked. "How do you know?"

"I just know," I said.

"He's right," Jake added. "Now that Farrell is warped, he won't stop. No matter what."

A flash of something that looked like pain darted across Fleet's face. He got up and circled the room. His heavy boots clunked over the wood floor. "You're right, Jake. As much as I hate agreeing with you on anything, destroying Farrell is the only way to stop him."

"Okay," I conceded, doubting it was possible to kill a powerful Transhuman like Farrell, but willing to do anything to help Dominique. "We kill Farrell. How will we do it?"

A wave of doubt and uncertainty swept through me as my question lingered in the air, the idea of facing off against Farrell seeming like a death wish.

"You fell on your knees back there at the church," Fleet said to Jake, suddenly changing the subject. "Why?"

Jake squirmed in his seat. "I think that associating with regular humans for so long and wearing this collar has weakened my power a little. That's why I carry a gun."

Fleet pointed to the metal around his neck, fury in his eyes. "This device is messing with my energy?" He zipped toward Jake, grabbed him by the top of his shirt, and jerked him to his feet. "You asshole!"

"No! It's only if you wear it too long!" Jake pleaded. "As in years too long. Not days, not even months."

Pushing them apart, I squeezed myself between them. "We'll never defeat Farrell like this!" Fleet stood down and Jake retreated to the couch. "You guys can fight all you want when this is over. Right now we need to figure out how to destroy Farrell. Got it?"

Jake muttered his assent while Fleet grunted. With that outburst behind us, I went back to racking my brain on how to kill a Transhuman. I remembered what had happened to Dominique when she had faced off against Tavion in the red desert. "She told me she faked her surrender," I said.

Jake perked up. "Come again?"

Fleet edged up to his seat. "That's right. I was there," he said. "Dominique agreed to a surrender, and then she, Farrell, and her parents ambushed Tavion. And you"—Fleet pointed to me—"you saved her when you touched that cross and freed Abigail's energy that brought Dominique back to life."

"And then she killed Tavion with that dagger," I said.

"Wait," Jake said. "She died, came back to life, and then killed Tavion with a dagger?"

"Yeah," I said. "Pretty much."

"Do either of you have the dagger?" Jake asked.

"No," Fleet answered.

Jake looked me squarely in the eye. "Can you bring her back to life again if she dies?"

"No."

"Then that plan sucks," Jake concluded.

Jake had a point, but I knew that an ambush of some sort was our only option. We just had to work through the details. Rubbing my tired eyes, I said, "Let's stay with this ambush notion, okay? Jake, these collars keep us hidden, right?"

"Yes, they disrupt our energy signal."

"So when we take them off, it's like standing in the middle of a giant bull's-eye?

"Yeah," Jake said. "Like jumping out of a hiding place."

"So the ambush is easy. What won't be easy is figuring out what to do once we are face-to-face with Farrell—" A yawn cut my sentence short, and I realized for the first time how utterly exhausted I was.

"Ambush it is," Fleet said. "We'll figure out the details later. Get some shut eye, Trent, before you pass out. And take care of that wound."

Easing myself up to my feet, ready to collapse with tiredness, I started making my way to the other side of the house where I had seen a second bedroom. My body moved slowly, my feet shuffled, and I could barely keep my eyes open.

"*Trent,*" a female voice whispered.

I stopped mid-step and looked around, wondering if Abigail had come for another visit, or maybe even Infiniti, but I didn't see anything.

"You okay?" Fleet asked.

Shaking my head slightly, as if to wake myself, I said, "I'm fine."

"*Trent.*"

This time I recognized the voice as Dominique's. My attention zoomed to her door. Was she communicating with me in some weird paranormal way? A lot of strange abilities and supernatural gifts ran in my family, so hearing her calling for me was not out of the realm of possibility.

I redirected my path. "I'm going to check on Dominique first." Approaching her door, I gave two soft raps. When she didn't answer, I slowly let myself in, prepared to find her in a state of distress, but hoping I was wrong because I couldn't take another loss like Infiniti's. None of us could.

"Please be okay," I said to myself, stepping into the pitch-black room, hoping for the best, but prepared for the worst.

Chapter Twenty

~ Dominique ~

Infiniti's pale face, her dark hair, the blood pooling on the marble floor beneath her small frame — that's all I could see as I lay on the hard bed. All I could feel inside my empty being was cutting guilt. I was responsible for the deaths of too many, maybe some I didn't even know about. But losing my dad, and now Infiniti, had done me in, and I was lost.

Shaking with remorse, I brought my hands up to my face. With the moonlight streaming through the window, I could see Infiniti's blood dried on my fingers, the metallic stench slowly fading. I should wash my hands, but these crimson stains were all I had left of her, my best friend who had stood by me no matter what, and I wanted to keep what traces of her I had left.

"Dude, please wash that off. It's gross!"

I knew that voice. Lowering my hands, I searched for Infiniti, but didn't see her. "Infiniti?" I whimpered. "Are you here?"

No response.

Realizing I was probably going mad, I went back to staring at my hands. Regardless of whether her voice was real or not, I knew she was right. I needed to get the dark splotches off.

Trudging over to the connected bathroom and switching on the light, I took a good look at myself in the mirror. Gaunt, pale, stringy hair, dark circles under my eyes, I resembled a walking corpse. Gazing down at my blood-soaked shirt, I embellished my assessment. I was more like a walking corpse that had been shot in the chest. Fatally wounded and left for dead.

Stripping down and tossing my dirty clothes in the tub, I found some soap, lathered my hands at the sink, and scrubbed at my skin with a washcloth I found hanging on the towel bar. Back and forth, over and over, I worked at my task until my hands were raw and my face covered in tears.

Looking up at my reflection, I said, "I can't do this."

This time, no one answered me.

Taking the small towel and rinsing it, I rubbed the cloth over my face, then cleaned my body. Shivering and sore all over, I rummaged through the linen closet and found a thin white sheet. I wrapped it around myself, and then shuffled back to the bed. Crawling under the covers, I lay on my back and gazed at the ceiling. Fleet, Trent, and Jake's arguing voices drifted into my room. Turning on my side, I covered my ears. I didn't want to hear them fighting over my fate because I didn't care anymore. None of it mattered. My dad and my best friend were dead. And I already knew what I had to do.

Kill Farrell.

"I hope you can, Dominique."

Sitting up with a start, I found myself on a bed of sand, the beach all around me. Blue lake water rippled ahead. Sunny warmth kissed my skin. Breathing in deep, I replaced the musty smell of the Galveston house with crisp, fresh Michigan air, realizing I must've fallen asleep.

A hand reached down for me. It was Farrell, helping me up. His sorrow-filled eyes studied mine. He stroked my check with his strong hand. "I'm sorry about Infiniti, babe."

I pressed his palm against my skin, wishing he didn't want to kill me, hoping I could end him first. "Me, too."

He lifted his other hand and cradled my face. "I love you, you know."

He brought his lips close to mine. Before they touched, I pulled away. "If you really love me, then don't do this."

He dropped his hands and slowly backed away from me. "It must be done, Dominique. I wish it didn't. But it must."

He turned and walked away from me, moving toward the lake. His image blurred with each step. His form became shimmery. His body broke into an array of gold-hued particles. When he reached the blue water, a gust of wind swept in and he floated away like a thousand crystal flecks caught in a windstorm.

"I love you, too, Farrell," I whispered.

There was no way he could hear me, but I needed to say it anyway. Longed for him to know that I knew he had no power over his actions, and that deep down I still loved him. Through all the death and all the sadness, he still had my heart. He always would.

Another puff of wind blew past. It carried a whisper that brushed at my ear.

"Kill me."

A lone tear tracked down my face. "I am. I will," I answered, finding myself following Farrell's footsteps to the water. The wind picked up. It tossed my hair around my face and tugged at the white sheet wrapped around my body.

Getting closer to the shore, I heard voices behind me. Pausing, I looked over my shoulder and saw my dad, my mom, Jan, Abigail, and Infiniti. "Keep going," they called out. "You're almost there."

Mom? Did seeing her with the others mean she was dead too? I wanted to ask, but stopped because it didn't matter. She had found my dad, and they were together.

"Don't stop, Dominique!" they said again.

As I stared at them, iridescent bursts caught my attention. Confused at first, I realized the phenomenon was coming from me, my body disintegrating like Farrell's had.

Dread seized me. I loved them all, but I wasn't ready to die yet. I had to kill Farrell.

I turned my thoughts to the one person who had never let me down, the one person who had always been there for me. I called out in my head, *"Trent, Trent, Trent."*

Somebody shook my shoulders. My eyes snapped open.

"Dominique?"

"Trent," I whispered, sitting up and hugging him tight, holding on for dear life. "I don't want to die."

He cradled the back of my head. "I don't want you to die either."

Locked in a desperate embrace I didn't want to break, I asked him to lay down with me. He kicked off his boots, took off his blood-stained shirt, and slid in beside me. I wrapped my arms around him and draped my leg over his. The soothing scent of soap that I always caught from him eased me. My hand moved across the bandage wrapped around his ribs. "Is this where you were shot?"

"Yes," he answered.

"Does it hurt?"

"A little."

"That nun was going to kill one of us no matter what, wasn't she?" I asked, thinking of the blond sister, wanting to murder her with my bare hands for taking Infiniti. "It was as if her destiny had to be fulfilled."

He traced my arm with his fingertips. "I suppose."

"If someone's destiny can't be avoided, then I'm going to die no matter what."

He pulled my chin so I could look at him fully. His blue eyes sparkled in the moonlight, sending a cascade of flutters in my stomach.

"Not if I can help it," he said.

My heart pounded. I had always had a connection with Trent, but the feelings I carried for Farrell ran deep and I knew Trent and I could never be together. But maybe being with Trent now would numb my pain and help me forget my heartache. I leaned in, working my hands up his smooth back and to his neck. "Do you remember back in that alley in 1930 when Infiniti said she wanted to have sex if she survived because she was still a virgin?"

"Yes," he whispered, looking at me with a deep longing. "I remember."

"I've never been with anyone either, Trent. And if this is the end for me, I want to feel love. Right now. With you."

His head dropped, and he pulled away from me. "You don't know what you're saying."

Threading my fingers into his hair, I pressed my body against his, desire building inside of me for him and only him. "Please, Trent," I begged. "I need you right now, more than ever." I brushed my lips against his. "I know you love me."

"I do," he whispered with a groan, kissing me long and deep, our tongues intertwining as he climbed on top of me. "I love you so much, Dominique," he breathed against my mouth. "I always have."

Locked in a passionate hold, mouths connected, I reached down to unbutton Trent's jeans when he stopped me. "I can't let you do this," he said, rolling off me and sitting on the edge of the bed. "You'd regret it, and so would I."

He was right, and I felt horrible for trying to use him. The void inside me expanded, swallowing me whole. "I'm ruined," I whispered, curling into a ball, wishing I could disappear forever.

He lay back down beside me and pulled me in. "No, you're not."

Desperately seeking comfort in his words, but not finding any, I drifted into a restless sleep.

***

A bright beam of light landed on my cheek. It warmed my skin, waking me with a gentle nudge. Shifting to my side, I studied Trent's beautiful face, his tan skin, his perfect nose, grateful he had talked me out of a mistake and stayed with me through the night. Watching as he slept peacefully, I wondered what would have happened between us if I were a normal girl without multiple past lives and a love that had lasted lifetimes. But then I stopped my thoughts short. That reality didn't exist. It never would. The only thing left for me was death.

Either mine or Farrell's.

Sensing I was awake, Trent smiled with his eyes still closed. "Good morning."

A blast of regret and embarrassment passed through me at how I had acted the night before. "Good morning," I said in a distant voice.

He propped himself up and looked at me. "What is it?"

"Nothing," I answered.

Sitting up all the way, he winced at the pain in his chest. "Don't do that, Dominique."

Kicking the covers off, and making sure my sheet was still secured around my body, I started riffling through the closets in hopes of finding clothes that fit. "I'm destined to die, and so are those connected to me." I paused. "And I almost ruined our friendship last night."

Yanking on his jeans, he came up behind me. "I actually think I ruined it when I told you —"

I turned and put my fingers on his lips. "I'm to blame for last night. Not you." I leaned my head on his bare chest. "I'm a giant mess."

He stroked my back. "I don't care."

"I do," I said, my voice trailing off.

"Then let's forget it," he said. "Okay?"

Breathing him in and not wanting to let go, I kissed his cheek, thinking he was too good for me. "Okay."

Dressed in fresh clothes that actually fit us pretty well, Trent and I joined the others. Fleet stood in the kitchen, drinking a cup of coffee. Jake sat on the couch and flipped through a book. "Hey," Jake said.

"Hey," I said back.

"There's coffee and donuts," Fleet said, avoiding eye contact with me. "If anyone is interested."

Trent squeezed my hand. "I'll serve us."

Pushing aside my breakdown, I went back to focusing on my destiny. Still reeling from the deaths in my life, I thought of the note I had written that said to kill Farrell and the two dreams I'd had of him. "He wants me to kill him."

Trent placed a plate of donuts and two mugs on the coffee table. "Who wants you to kill him?"

166

Fleet moved in closer, his death ray stare on me.

"Farrell," I answered.

"How do you know?" Jake asked.

"I saw him in a dream. Two actually, and he told me."

"What?" Jake asked. "He couldn't physically find you with that collar on, but he's still connected enough to you that he can appear in your dreams?" He rubbed his head. "Amazing. Your link to him must be powerful."

"He tracked you in your dreams?" Trent asked, his question laced with worry and concern and a hint of hurt that only I heard. "Can he harm you there? Are you at risk?"

"No, he doesn't want to hurt me. He's not even angry or scary. He's just... sad."

"It doesn't matter what he is," Fleet said. "He needs to die, and I think we all agree on that, right?"

"Right," everyone said.

"Then here's the plan," Fleet announced. "We remove our collars, let him find us, and then shoot him up with enough energy he'll explode."

"Disintegrate," I said, recalling my dreams, thinking that Farrell had been *showing* me how to kill him. Then I remembered that I too had broken into tiny little pieces. Did that mean we both had to die?

"What is it?" Trent asked.

"Nothing," I said, deciding to keep that detail of my dream to myself because it didn't change anything. Steeling my resolve, ready to do whatever needed to be done to finish this, I said, "We trap him, we kill him. It's settled. When?"

"Well," Jake answered. "We need to run some tests on the collars, and Fleet, Trent, and I need to practice connecting our energy streams. I'd say a week. Maybe less."

Chatter filled the room over the plan, but I kept quiet. Relieved at having a course of action, ready to die or move on with my life, and then I made another decision.

I was going to do everything in my power to make sure Trent lived.

Chapter Twenty-One

~ Trent ~

Doing my best to focus on our plan to end Farrell while trying to push aside what I had said to Dominique in the bedroom, I thought of Jake's statement about needing to test the collars. With everyone agreeing on the trap-and-kill method, I circled back to the metal devices.

"Hey," I said to Jake. "What do you mean about testing these?" I tapped my own metal choker.

Like an eager scientist explaining his favorite experiment, Jake said, "The collars disrupt our energy force and act like a cloaking device. When we remove them, we're exposed again. What I don't know is how long it will take for the shielding effect to disappear. It's an unknown variable."

"What? You didn't say that last night," Fleet seethed.

"I know I didn't. It was something I thought about late last night." Seeing Fleet's scowl, he let out a nervous laugh. "It's not that big of a deal. We just need to test it. That's all."

"How?" Dominique asked.

"We remove one of them and see how long it takes for Farrell to appear."

Fleet pounded his fist on the couch. "That's a pretty damn big piece of information you left out. Are you keeping anything else from us?"

Anger sparked in Jake's eyes. "No, I'm not keeping anything from anyone. By the way, we're on the same team, and I'm really getting sick and tired of your bullshit, man! Enough is enough. So back the fuck off!"

Jake and Fleet were on their feet now, ready to exchange blows. Dominique edged between them while I held Fleet's arms. "He's right," she said to Fleet. "You need to stop."

Fleet jerked away from me. Anguish dashed across his face, and I started feeling sorry for the guy. He was in love with Dominique in first life, lost her to Farrell, and I was pretty sure he thought Dominique and I had just been together. I'd be pissed, too.

"How exactly do we test the collars?" Dominique asked, changing the subject. "How does that work?"

Jake lifted his backpack. He took out an extra collar, followed by a thin object that looked like a nail file. "The collar is made of metal." He ran his fingers around it. "Inside are pointed barbs that penetrate into the skin." He took the file. "This is a piece of plastic. All you have to do is work it between your skin and the collar and disconnect one of the barbs from your neck. Once you do that, the collar will fall off."

Jake passed around the plastic. Soft, thin and rubbery, I pulled and found it actually really tough. "That sounds easy enough," I said. "But what about the other part? The waiting for Farrell to find us part?"

"I was thinking we could go some place far away, someplace deserted, like an empty field or something. One of us can take off the collar. When Farrell appears, we slam it back on and get out of there."

"Using Transhuman powers?" Dominique asked.

"Yeah," Jake said. "We'd have to."

"You hardly have any power," Fleet said to Jake. "So you're out. And you"—he looked to me—"have no idea how to use yours. I'm going alone."

"Whoa, hold up," I said. "I may not know how to tap into what I can to do, but you're gonna need back up."

"Trent's right," Jake said to Fleet. "Plus, he's powerful. The most powerful Transhuman I've ever seen. His stream back there at the church could've lit up the entire Eastern Seaboard."

Dominique paced the room, twirling a strand of long hair. "I don't like it, but it makes sense." She eyed me and Fleet nervously. "The two of you will be stronger together."

Jake put the extra collar back in his pack. He handed Fleet the plastic. Fleet thumbed it, then shoved it in his front jeans pocket. He marched over to me. "You ready?"

"What? You want to leave right now?" I had no problem with the mission, but Fleet caught me off guard with wanting to leave so quickly.

"Why not? I even have the perfect place in mind," Fleet said.

I let out a breath. "Yeah, okay, let's go."

"Wait!" Dominique called out, coming over to us. She placed one hand on my arm and the other on Fleet's. "Be careful. And please come back."

"Of course," I said, trying my best to sound reassuring.

Fleet took a hold of my wrist. His gray aura raced out of his hands, lacing around and up my arm. The floor beneath our feet opened up, and I slipped into a free fall. My stomach dipped, and before I could figure out which way was up, my feet thudded onto crunchy ground—

snow-covered ground in the middle of the woods. A two-story log cabin came into view.

"We're back at the Boardman?" I asked Fleet, looking around and studying the landscape. The last time I was here we were attacked by a group of Tainted. Eyeing the skies, I waited for our enemies to explode from the clouds, but nothing happened. "Is it safe for us to be here?"

"We're safe, until we take off this collar, that is." He made his way to the cabin, our boots thudding on the soft snow.

"Why did you pick this place?" I asked.

"I wanted to check on my people. See if Richard and Sue are..." I could tell he wanted to say dead, but instead said, "okay."

Approaching the back door, we saw fresh piles of snow all the way up to the porch. Nobody had been in or out of the house in a long time. Fleet knocked. "Hello?"

No response.

He tried the door. Finding it open, we let ourselves in. The stench of burnt wood filled my nostrils and I had to cover my nose with my sleeve. Black stripes of char streaked the inside of the foyer.

"Shit," Fleet said. In a daze, we made our way to the heart of the home. Every shred of furniture, the very walls and the ceiling itself, had been burned to a crisp. Fleet let out a howl of rage and punched his fist into the nearest wood beam.

Instead of saying anything, I went outside and left him alone with his agony. I knew his grief extended beyond the loss of Richard and Sue, and I wondered how much more he could take.

I shivered in the cold until Fleet emerged. From where I stood to the side, I could see his eyes were bloodshot, his shoulders hunched. Catching sight of me, he straightened his back and tramped my way. "Let's go out to the open space and do what we need to do and get the hell out of here."

Teeth chattering from the cold and hands shoved in my pockets, I followed him down the small path between the naked pines to the spot that Richard and Sue had used for a fire pit. With a flick of his hand, he started a roaring blaze.

"Thanks," I muttered, getting close and warming myself. "And for what it's worth, I'm sorry about everything that's happened to you, man. I really am. All of it."

"Don't be," he said. He wanted no sympathy from me.

"So," I said, feeling uncomfortable and not knowing what to say. "How are we going to do this?"

He took the thin plastic out of his pocket. "The second I get my collar off, you start counting. When Farrell appears, I'll slam it back on, hold on to you, and I'll get us out of here."

"Your collar? Not mine?"

"Nope, not yours. I have no idea what'll happen when this comes off, so it's better if I do it."

I moved closer to him, wanting to be near for a quick exit. "Okay. And if something goes wrong?"

"We deal with it," he said. Puffs of vapor came out of his mouth. He positioned the file at his neck. "Ready?"

I inched even closer. "Ready."

Letting out a long breath, he wedged the plastic between his skin and the collar, stretching his neck to the side. He stabbed the file around until a snapping sound filled the air. The collar unclasped and dropped. Fleet snatched it before it hit the ground, and I started counting.

One, two, three, four, five, six, seven, eight, nine —

A blast of lightning battered into the dirt. The force of the energy connecting with the earth flung Fleet and me into the air, hurtling us away from each other. Crashing to the ground, I lost my sense of orientation for a few seconds before I spotted Farrell and Fleet standing face-to-face about ten feet away from me. Same height, same muscular build, same fists clenched at their sides.

Doing a double-take, I realized Fleet's hands were empty. *Crap.* He must've dropped the piece of metal when the strike occurred. I stayed flat on the ground, my body pressed against the snow. Playing dead and trying not to make a sound, I eyed the white landscape, searching for the silver collar, knowing I needed to get it back on Fleet so we could escape.

"You're no match for me," Farrell said.

"Maybe," Fleet admitted. "But that doesn't mean I'm not gonna try to kick your ass. But before we get to it, I have to know something. Why did you do it? Why did you betray me?"

Darting my gaze across the area, frantically looking for the collar, I noticed the index finger of one of Fleet's hands pointing behind his brother. Craning my neck, I saw the smooth, silver device poking out from a clump of snow by Farrell's foot.

Great.

"My main objective was to protect the Marked One," Farrell answered. "Anything else that happened was secondary and unintentional."

Fleet's fingers started counting down from five, letting me know when to charge for the collar. With my heart beating at a rapid fire pace, I tensed my muscles, ready to spring from my position.

"One more question, bro," Fleet said, his fingers at

three. "What would you say if I told you Dominique didn't love you? That she never did?"

Farrell took a step back, Fleet's finger count ended, and I sprang into action.

Blasts of electricity exploded from Farrell and Fleet, smoky plumes filled the air, and I dove for the device. Sliding across the cold slush, I stopped short, my fingertips inches away from our ticket home. I stretched out as far as I could and nearly had it in my grasp when a boot slammed down on my hand.

Letting out a grunt, I turned to see Farrell looming over me. Beyond him, I saw Fleet trapped in a sizzling bubble of vapor.

"Did you lose something?" Farrell asked.

My brain calculated everything I had been told about Transhumans, zeroing in on that moment when I had transported our group to 1930. If I had enough strength for a move like that, then I knew I could get us out of this situation. If I could get the collar, penetrate that bubble and grab Fleet, I could get us out of there. I just had to distract Farrell. But how?

"Dominique's inside the cabin," I said, jerking my chin in the direction of Richard and Sue's place. "She's wearing the collar, so you can't tell. But she's in there." Farrell's eyes hardened with deadly determination, his stare moving to the empty house. "Put me in the bubble with Fleet and go see for yourself. If I'm lying, you can come back and kill us."

Going along with my lie, Fleet yelled, "Why did you tell him!" And then he hollered, "Dominique, run!"

Overcome with his desire to end her, Farrell vanished into thin air.

"Shit," Fleet said. "Hurry, before he comes back."

I bolted for the shield, collar in hand, my body aglow with my blue aura. Making contact, my body sizzled through with ease, a tingly feeling coursing through me as I crossed over.

Fleet grabbed the collar. He had started to put it on when Farrell zapped into view on the other side of the force field. Fire lit his eyes, his jaw clenching in fury at our deception. The necklace snapped into place around Fleet's neck. He latched onto my arm as his vapor oozed out. The ground below us started to open. But not fast enough.

Farrell raised his arms. Like the beginning of a lightning storm, sparks crackled from his fingertips, and I had mere seconds to act. I raised my hands, determined to deflect his attack. Focusing on my blue energy, I thought of my parents, my grandparents, and even my great-grandparents. "You can't hurt me," I said.

Farrell unleashed his strength. Thick bolts of power screamed out of his hands. The blast met my palms. Instead of incinerating me, the explosions ricocheted off and bounced into the sky. As the array of lights dashed across the heavens, Fleet and I slipped out of view and landed on the floor in the beach house.

"Trent!" Dominique raced over to me, followed by Jake.

Peering over at Fleet, I saw his clothes were singed, his face covered in ash, as if he had just survived a forest fire. I looked down at myself. My clothes were singed too. When I brought my hands up, I saw that they were covered in blood.

"Your face," Jake said with alarm. "What the hell happened?"

My cheeks were warm, but other than that, I couldn't feel anything. "What is it?" I asked.

Tears sprang to Dominique's eyes. She covered her mouth.

My gut sank. "Is it that bad?"

Dominique looked at Fleet. "Can you help him?"

Scrambling to my feet, I stumbled to the bathroom. A person with bloodied burn marks covering every inch of their face stared back at me. I shuddered, feeling sorry for the person, wondering how he'd gotten in the house, when I noticed his eyes were blue. Bright blue. Like mine.

Sickening realization dawned on me.

Bile came up my throat.

I was looking in the mirror. And the burned face was mine.

Chapter Twenty-Two

~ Dominique ~

Jake and I waited in silence for Fleet and Trent to return from testing the collars. Jake fiddled with the extra devices in his pack while I spent my time outside. Staring blankly at the ocean, I thought of Infiniti, wishing she'd come back somehow, wondering what it really meant for her to be on her first life. Then I thought of Trent and the way he had exposed his heart to me. I'd be devastated if he didn't return, and I prayed for him to be okay. After a while, Jake joined me on the porch.

He sat in a rocking chair next to me and sighed. "Nice weather."

The wild changes in the Houston weather didn't surprise me anymore. One day it could be freezing, then the next warm enough for shorts. Today was definitely a shorts day. The sun shone bright. A warm breeze circulated the air. In spite of the heat, I stuck with jeans and the long-sleeved, black shirt I had found in the closet. I couldn't shake the chill in my bones.

"I guess it's nice," I answered.

Jake's chair creaked as he rocked back and forth. A light wind whistled through the porch screen, filling the air with a lonely tune. "Love complicates everything, doesn't it?" Jake said.

My love for Farrell, the way Trent felt about me, and the relationship I supposedly had with Fleet in first life I didn't remember made everything difficult. "Yeah."

"Do you want to know why I left the group back in first life? Why I turned my back on our mission?"

I turned to face him and noticed the pain in his eyes. "I thought you said you were scared."

"No, I wasn't scared."

"Then why did you say that?"

Tears glistened in his eyes. His rocking stilled. "I fell in love with an amazing girl. Long brown hair, deep brown eyes. Her name was Olivia. We met in a coffee shop. Fleet was with me that day, but he didn't notice how I looked at her, or how she pretended not to notice me."

He smiled as if remembering that moment. "I went back there every day after that, ordered my coffee, chatted with Olivia. We fell in love so slowly I didn't even recognize it at first. It wasn't until our band of Pures had to go in into hiding that I knew Olivia had me, all of me. So I left everything and everyone to be with her."

He continued rocking, his gaze straight ahead, staring at the beach.

"What happened?" I asked.

"We did what normal people do. We got married. We got jobs. I tried to accelerate my aging to match hers, but I couldn't. Eventually I had to tell her about me, and you know what? She didn't care. She said we'd make it work as long as we could. And we did, but for me it wasn't nearly long enough. I ended up watching her die, Dominique, an old lady in my arms."

He wiped his eyes. "I was messed up after that. Big

time. I didn't want to live, didn't want to fight. Didn't want to be a Transhuman. Didn't want to do anything. That's why I bailed."

Choking up at the details of his past, I grabbed his arm, imagining his loss. "I'm so sorry, Jake."

He put his hand on top of mine. "Me, too."

An energy pulse streamed inside the house. The floor shook. Jake and I ran inside and saw Fleet and Trent on the floor. Tufts of smoke filled the air around them. Their clothes were burned. When I saw Trent's face, I froze in horror and covered my mouth.

"Is it that bad?" Trent asked me.

I had no words. His burns were so severe I barely recognized him.

"Can you help him?" I asked Fleet.

Trent rushed to the bathroom. Afraid of what he'd see in the mirror, I hesitated before joining him and hung back with Fleet. "Please, you have to help him." I clawed at his sleeve. "You have to."

"I'm not a great healer like Farrell, but I'll do my best."

Fleet and I entered the bathroom with caution. Trent gripped the sink with his bloodied hands. His head hung low. "Can you fix me?" he asked Fleet.

"Yeah," Fleet said. "I think I can. Let's get you on the bed."

Leading Trent gently by his arm, I directed him to the bedroom where we had slept the night before. He eased onto the mattress, and I slipped off his boots. "Are you in pain?" I asked.

"No. In fact, I can't feel anything at all."

"The pain will come later," Jake said, joining us with an armful of throw pillows. "I have experience with third-

degrees burns. We need to elevate his hands and his head."
I took the pillows from Jake and placed one under each of
Trent's forearms and a few behind his head.

"I'll get towels," Fleet said, disappearing into the
bathroom and coming back with a few washcloths. He
placed one on each of Trent's hands, and then draped one
on his face. "Trent, I'm going to cool your body. It will put
you in a comatose state to help speed up the healing
process. My energy will mix with yours while you're
sleeping and regenerate your skin, okay?"

Trent swallowed hard. "Okay."

Fleet positioned himself beside the bed. He hovered
his hands over Trent's body. His gray power seeped out,
drifting out onto Trent like a light, misty rain. A few
droplets landed on my arm and I shivered. The drizzle was
ice cold. The air in the room grew frigid, turning my nose
into an icicle and my breath into vapor.

After staying in that position for a good five minutes,
and transforming the bedroom into a meat locker, Fleet
lowered his hands and collapsed onto his knees. I started to
help him. "Don't touch me," he said.

Stung by his resentment toward me, even though I
should've been used to it, I withdrew and left the room.
Jake followed me. "You think Trent will be okay?"

"I hope so," I answered, trying not to let on how Fleet
affected me.

Fleet tramped into the room, startling me. "I'm going
to make a run to the store to get some ointment for Trent."

"Wait," Jake said. "Let me go. Trent might wake up
and need help, and I can't do what you can do."

I didn't want to be alone with Fleet so I blurted out,
"I'll go with you."

"Nah, you better stay, too. If Trent wakes, he'll really
want to see you. I'll be back."

Fleet tossed him the car keys and Jake left, leaving me alone with my first love. The guy I had wanted to marry, yet didn't remember in the least. With Farrell, even though I had no memory of our past, surges of deep emotions filtered through me, moments of our time together painting the back of my mind. With Fleet, there was nothing.

After several long minutes of ignoring me, Fleet went to the kitchen. Combing through the pantry, he pulled out a bottle of whisky and poured himself a glass. Compelled to somehow clear the air between us, I joined him at the kitchen counter.

"I don't need the company," he said.

"I know. But I do."

He snickered. "Yeah, you sure do. With just about any guy who crosses your path."

I slammed my hand across his face and then stared at him, shocked that I had assaulted him like that. "You don't know me," I asserted.

He took a swig of his drink as if the blow were a mere pat. "Oh yeah, I know you. Better than you think, Dominique. And you used to know me."

My anger waned, edged out by pity. "Listen, Fleet. I know what we were to each other back in first life, and I'm sorry I don't remember any of it. I really am. But you need to know I'm not that person any more. I haven't been for a long time. You can't be mad at me for not remembering the past. It's not fair."

He downed the alcohol. "You're right. It's not fair, but my memories of you kept me sustained for decades as I delved deeper and deeper undercover with Tavion. Holding on to you kept me alive. So you'll have to forgive me if I find it challenging to let go of what we had." He poured himself another drink. "Now leave me."

I started to walk away from him, but changed my mind. "I hope you weren't like this with Infiniti."

He clanked his glass down. "I wasn't."

The door swung open and Jake entered with a handful of plastic bags. "I've got tons of ointment, plus something to eat." He unloaded his supply run on the kitchen table and he and Fleet started sifting through the contents.

"So what happened to you guys?" Jake asked Fleet. "When you tested the collars. How did Trent get burned?"

"We went back to the Boardman," Fleet said.

"The Boardman?" Jake asked. "Richard and Sue's place?"

"I wanted to check on them, see if they were still there."

"Were they?" I asked, hopeful that somehow they were safely in their comfy log house, remembering how they told me I had called them Aunt Sue and Uncle Richard.

"No," Fleet said. "By the looks of the house, they were wiped out."

My hands shook as my world fell apart just a little bit more. "They're dead?"

Fleet's jaw clenched. "Yes."

"Man, poor Richard and Sue," Jake said. "Then what?"

"I removed the collar, and Farrell showed up, just like you said he would. He came so fast he caught me off guard and there was a scuffle. If not for Tent, we'd both have been obliterated."

"I knew it!" Jake said excitedly. "He's so filled with energy he doesn't even have to know what to do to wield it. It just works!"

"His face is burned to a crisp, Jake. I wouldn't exactly call that working," I said.

"No, of course not. I didn't mean it that way. But I do think he's our secret weapon." Jake stared in the direction of Trent's room. "With him on our side, with all that raw power, I think we can really kill Farrell."

"Well right now, our secret weapon needs some medicine," I said.

On cue, Fleet started inspecting the creams. He palmed two yellow tubes. "These should do," he said.

Jake stayed in the kitchen and Fleet and I returned to the frigid room. We removed the towels from Trent's hands and face. Fleet passed me the cream. Squirting the contents of the tubes onto my fingers, I liberally applied the salve to Trent's wounds. Running my fingers over his scorched skin, I fought to keep my cool. Was it possible for his face to heal? Would he ever look the same?

"He'll be fine," Fleet said.

Pausing, I eyed Fleet. "Can you—?"

"Read your mind? No. But I know your expressions well enough that people often thought I could. We sometimes even made a game of it."

I could tell he wanted me to probe him further about the memory, or ask him something about how things used to be with us, but I didn't. What for? It would only make things worse for him. And for me too.

With one tube emptied, I opened the other and went to work on Trent's face. It felt as if my fingers were running over a rocky surface. Crevice-filled, thick, and hard. His perfectly tan face had been destroyed.

Fleet started making his way out of the room so I could be alone with Trent. He paused at the door, lingering for a minute. "I didn't mean to lose my cool."

"I didn't mean to lose my memory."

He smirked. "Fair enough. But you need to know something." He paused and looked down at his feet. "I will never forget you."

Fleet left me alone with more pain in my heart than ever. With the contents of the tubes emptied, and Trent's injuries smothered with the healing ointment, I slumped down to the ground and watched over him in the igloo-like environment. Wrapped up in extra blankets that Jake had delivered, I stayed in the bedroom and waited for a miraculous recovery. Every now and again I checked Trent's pulse for signs of life. Sometimes it was so faint I had to poise my hand over his face to feel the air coming out of his nose. Getting up only for bathroom breaks and refusing offers of food, I waited. Minutes turned to hours. The day turned to night. And I kept watch.

Deep into the night, Jake crept into the room, his feet padding quietly on the wood floor. He joined me on the ground where I sat leaning against the wall.

"You can't keep this up, Dom."

In a trance-like daze, I said, "Yes I can."

Jake started watching my patient, too. We stared at his still form in silence. The rise and fall of Trent's chest was so slight, it was a wonder he was getting air into his lungs.

"What are you watching for?" Jake asked in a hushed voice.

"I don't want to be asleep if he dies. Couldn't bear it if he left this world alone." My words came out soft and slow because I was so tired.

"What?" Jake scooted closer to me, pressing his back against the wall. He linked his arm with mine. "He's not going to die."

I could barely keep my eyes open. Had a hard time keeping my chin up. "How do you know?"

"His injuries are serious, but not life-threatening." He moved my head onto his shoulder and patted my head. "Now sleep, okay? If anything happens, I'll wake you."

Exhaustion took away my will to resist his offer. My muscles loosened. My eyes closed. The last thing on my mind before I passed out was death.

Mine.

"Wake up."

Farrell's voice whispered in my ear. I wanted to get up and talk to him. Longed to see his face. Kiss his lips. But my heavy slumber wrestled me down and wouldn't let me.

"Dominique, wake."

My eyes fluttered open. A face hovered in front of me. It was Farrell.

"I need to talk to you," he said.

Scanning my surroundings, I realized I was back at Elk Rapids beach. This time it was dark out. The sky was filled with gray clouds, and only sprinklings of stars shone through the puffy matter.

"Why do you keep coming to me in my dreams?" I asked.

He held me close, his expression serious. "You have to let go of your hurt, turn off your emotions, and get ready to kill me." He waited for me to say something, but my sleeping brain was too muddled. "I'm coming, Dominique. Soon." He shook me by my shoulders. "Do you hear me?"

His words slowly sank through. "I hear you, but I don't know if I can do it."

He winced. "You can. I know it, and you know it. You just have to push through your pain."

Heartache over what he had done to my loved ones

sent tears to my eyes, but I blinked them away because I knew he was right.

He pressed his forehead against mine. "Turn off your emotions. Okay? No matter what." He brushed his lips against mine. "It's the only way."

Our bodies locked in a desperate embrace. Pushing into him, we kissed slow and deep, and I knew it was for the last time.

Chapter Twenty-Three

~ Trent ~

The smell of coffee drifted around my head. Penetrating my sense of smell, it sent a grumble through my stomach. Lying still and catching my bearings, I realized my eyes were wide open. A cloudy, white film hazed my vision. A jolt of panic numbed me. Had I gone blind like my grandmother? Then I remembered the confrontation with Farrell, the burns on my body, and the white towel on my face. Did the fiery blast from Farrell take my sight? Struggling to move my stiff arms and pull off the sheath, I jumped when a hand touched mine.

"It's okay," Dominique said. "It's me. I got it."

She gently folded the covering into a tiny square, and then lifted it from my eyes. Her face came into view. The tips of her long hair hovered inches from me. Instead of looking terrified, she sighed with relief. "Much better," she said.

Jake popped up behind her. "Oh yeah," he said, moving in. He studied my face as if I were under a microscope. "The burns are healing nicely."

I brought my hands up for inspection. The once bloodied-looking clubs were now clean, the thick, bulbous charring reduced to a thin leathery texture. I swung my legs over the side of the bed, pausing when I realized the frigid air in the room had returned to a normal temperature. "I want to see my face."

I stood on rubbery legs, and Jake and Dominique swooped in to steady me. "Nice and slow," Dominique said. "You've been out for a week."

My mind worked to comprehend that I had been asleep for so many days. "A week?"

"Yep," Jake answered. "We would've kept you under longer but, you know, we've got stuff to do."

"Trap and kill," I uttered, remembering full well we had a task to perform. "I haven't forgotten."

Alone in the bathroom, I timidly approached the mirror. Keeping my gaze down, it took me a while to raise my head and meet my reflection. Red and raw, my face looked like it had baked too long in the sun. Running my damaged fingers over the aftermath of the scorching by Farrell, I wondered if I would heal more, or if this was it. And then I supposed looking like this was better than being dead.

After taking my time in the bathroom, I joined the others. Dominique and Jake waited by the door of the bedroom. Fleet joined them. "Welcome to the land of the living," Fleet said. "Now let's get to work. Meet me in the kitchen."

Jake handed me a cup of coffee. I waved it away, feeling too dehydrated for caffeine. "I'd actually like some water."

"I'll get it," Dominique said.

She hurried to the kitchen, and I followed behind her at a slower pace. "So, is this it?" I asked Fleet, my mind still on my injuries. "Or will my wounds get better?"

"They should continue to improve," he said. "In time, you'll barely be able to see the scars."

Time... I wondered if I really had any time. If any of us did.

"We also got you some more creams," Jake offered. "To help."

"Thanks," I said, sitting on the edge of the sofa and taking the bottle of water Dominique handed me. To me, it seemed only mere hours had passed, yet it had been multiple days. "A week," I said again, almost not believing it. "What did you all do while I was out?"

"I've been working on strengthening my energy output," Jake said.

"And we've been mapping out the kill," Fleet said. "We've decided to set the trap for Farrell back at the Boardman since nobody is there and the area is secluded."

"I had wanted to finish things here, but with the days warming up, we think it best to leave Galveston," Dominique said. "To avoid beach-goers."

They were throwing so much information at me at once, my head started pounding. But they were right. We needed a more private location, and we needed to be swift. Waiting around would only makes things worse and put more people at risk.

Steadying myself, I gripped the couch cushion. "When do we do it? I'm ready to finish this."

"We are, too," Dominique said. Something in her demeanor told me she had changed while I slept. She didn't look broken anymore. Instead, her gaze held steady. Her voice rang strong. "Farrell keeps visiting me in my dreams, and his message is always the same. He tells me he's going to kill me, and he warns that he's coming. Now that you're up, we need to prepare so we can strike first."

Because my face felt foreign and stiff, I kept dribbling water out of my mouth. I blotted my face on my sleeve and used the moment to try to hide that I was incensed at the idea of Farrell still having a hold on Dominique. Instead of focusing on the agreed upon plot and the accelerated timeline, I zeroed in on her dreams. She had dreamed of him before, and apparently hadn't stopped. I was pissed. "He asks for you to kill him, and then says he's on his way? Is that it?"

Her eyes shifted, and I knew she was holding something back. "Yes, that's it."

I wanted to challenge her, but I had been out of it for a while and didn't know if I should, especially in front of the others. So I decided to let it go and bring it up later.

"We need to get your strength up," Fleet said to me, arms crossed. "If we're to face off against Farrell and succeed, we all need to be at the top of our game."

My head started spinning. My body felt weak. I was anything but at the top of my game, yet I knew they needed me. "I agree, and I'm all in, but give me today, okay? I'll be better tomorrow."

Fleet took an impatient breath. "Fine. We'll start our training tomorrow, first thing. And hey…" He waited until I met his eyes. "Thanks for saving my ass."

"Sure," I said. "Anytime."

Fleet left the room and went outside. Jake retreated to one of the back bedrooms. Dominique stayed with me in the den. Alone with her, I relaxed my tense muscles and eased myself into the couch. "I see things haven't changed much around here," I said to Dominique. "Fleet is still in a permanent bad mood, and Jake continues to be elusive."

"Fleet's been through a lot," she said, defending him. "Jake, too. Besides, they're on our team, personality defects and all."

"I guess we all carry baggage of some sort," I responded, taking another sip of water. "What I can't understand is you. You've changed since I've been asleep."

She didn't flinch, a dead giveaway that she knew exactly what I was talking about. She still tried to pretend. "What do you mean?"

"Are you serious?" I placed the water bottle on the coffee table. "Don't tell me you're oblivious to your change in disposition."

Offended, she said, "I'm fighting for my life, Trent. I don't have time to be emotional." I stared at her, as if she were a complete stranger. She broke eye contact, and her expression softened. "Seeing your injuries and watching you on that bed, I thought I was going to lose you. Like Infiniti. I'm tired of losing people, and I can't take another blow like that. I can't." Her eyes teared up. "Emotions make us weak. Weakness leads to casualties. If we can put our feelings aside, we can win. I know it."

Every word coming out of her made sense, but they didn't exactly sound like they were hers. She had to have picked them up from Farrell and his frequent nighttime visits.

"This is coming from Farrell, isn't it?"

She threw me a death stare. "No. It's coming from me. I'm ready to fight. Aren't you?"

"Of course I am," I said.

"Good, because I need you."

The last time she had said she needed me was when we were in bed. Our passionate kiss from that night replayed in my mind, and I wondered if she even remembered what I had said to her. Thinking of her fondness for the beach, believing a change of scenery would be good for her and for me, I said, "Let's go for a walk. I could use the exercise and the fresh air."

Her eyes lit up a bit. "Okay."

We made our way across the sandy dunes, kicked off our shoes, rolled up our jeans, and stood ankle deep in the frothy water. My feet sank into the thick, wet sand. The sun filtered through the clouds. The cool breeze hugged our bodies.

"How's your face?"

Instead of the sun irritating my skin like I thought it would, the rays invigorated me on a cellular level, lifting my spirits. "It's fine." I raised my chin and breathed in the salty air, surprised when Dominique took my hand and laced her fingers with mine.

"You really scared me, Trent."

Everything about her captivated me. Her long hair that glittered with different hues of amber and gold in the sunlight, her eyes that changed from light to dark green depending on what she wore, the spray of freckles on the bridge of her nose that you didn't notice until you got up close. If only Farrell didn't have a hold on her. She released my hand.

"I didn't mean to scare you, Dominique."

We started walking down the shore, our feet splashing through the tides. "I know," she said. Spotting something shiny, she scooped up the treasure and inspected it. "What's this?" she asked, holding out the white, opaque fragment.

I took her finger and brushed it across the glossy surface. "It's sea glass."

"Sea glass?"

"Yeah. No sea glass in Michigan?"

"No, only rocks and stones."

I thought of the Petoskey stone she had given me for Christmas that I had returned to her in 1930, wondering what had happened to it. "Sea glass is glass that's been in the ocean for so long that the waves have pounded away the sharp edges until it comes out smooth like this."

She held it up to the light and inspected it. "It's beautiful."

I wanted to wrap my arm around her, pull her in, and tell her how beautiful she was, but I didn't.

As if sensing my thoughts, she backed away from me. She gave the white glass a toss into the ocean, watching it plop into the waves. "I have to turn off my emotions. My feelings. All of it. Or we'll never win."

"Emotions don't make us weak, Dominique. Besides, what do emotions have to do with anything?" I kicked at the sand. "This is about Farrell and your dreams, isn't it? You're holding something back from them, aren't you?"

She didn't answer.

"I don't get how you can still be bound to Farrell after everything he's done to you. He's killed so many, Dominique. Doesn't that mean anything to you?"

"It's not him," she said, defending Farrell. "And it doesn't matter anymore because I know what I have to do. So drop it."

I shoved my hands in his pockets. "Do you think you can really kill him if given the chance?"

She stared down at her sand covered feet. "I have to." She brushed her hair out of her face, but avoided eye contact with me and I knew I had struck a chord. "I'm going back to the house." I had started to follow her when she stopped me. "Alone."

I watched her disappear over the dunes and out of view.

Sinking down to the sand, I sat and stared out at the Gulf of Mexico. Powerful waves crashed up to the shoreline, then slipped back into the tide. A V-shaped formation of seagulls squawked by, swooping close to me for a bite, cawing for food. With nothing to offer them, they continued on their journey, leaving me to contemplate my predicament. Dominique's words echoed in my head.

Emotions make us weak.

I picked up a long, dark, oyster shell and started tracing the sand. Dominique had a point. We had lost too many, and we needed to stop that deadly trend. If she wanted to hide her emotions, then I would too. It was time to put aside my feelings for her, permanently, so that I could help her as a friend. It was up to me — to all of us — to give Dominique the chance to live out her final life.

No matter what, at any cost, we needed Farrell to be the final death.

Chapter Twenty-Four

~ Dominique ~

Marching away from Trent, rattled by his words, I told myself that he didn't know what he was talking about. How dare he say that the deaths of my loved ones didn't mean anything to me! And why did he have to make it so hard for me to turn off my feelings? At the edge of the dunes, I grabbed my shoes and kicked his, and then trudged up to the beach house.

He didn't mean to hurt you.

I spun around, looking for Infiniti, but didn't see her. Shaking my head and telling myself I was hearing things, I trotted up the stairs to the house and made a beeline for the room that I had been sleeping in. I flopped on the bed, crossed my arms, and huffed.

Studying the plastic, glow-in-the-dark stars pasted to the ceiling, I forced myself to slow my breathing. I had to turn off my emotions so I could win. But could I? I grabbed a pillow and slammed it on my face.

A light tap sounded at my door. "What!" I shouted, wanting to be left alone.

"Can I come in?" It was Jake

After a long pause I said, "Sure."

The door creaked open, and Jake poked his head in timidly. "What the heck is up with you?" He came in all the way and shut the door behind him. "You stomped in so loudly I thought we were being attacked."

The more time I spent with Jake, the closer I grew to him. Like a true best friend, I had opened up to him during our vigil watching over Trent. He shared stories about his time with Olivia, and I revealed my deep love for Farrell and attraction for Trent. Having him around was like therapy.

"So what gives? What's got you so worked up?"

I didn't have a problem confiding in Jake, but the idea of rehashing my conversation with Trent made me sick to my stomach. "It's nothing I can't handle."

He fiddled with the frayed edges of the comforter. "I saw the way you looked at Trent when he asked you about your dreams of Farrell. Is there something about those dreams you're not telling me?"

I had told Fleet and Jake about the dreams and Farrell's message, but I never told them the part about kissing Farrell, or Farrell and me dissolving into dust. The same way I had withheld that information from Trent. "No."

"Are you sure?"

Someone knocked, saving me from telling Jake another lie.

"Come in," I said.

Fleet opened the door but stayed at the threshold. "Trent wants to start prep today."

Shocked at Trent's change of heart, it took me a few seconds to find my words. "He does?"

"Yep." Fleet rubbed his hands. "It's show time."

Trent waited for us out in the main room. In just that

short time that he was on the beach, his face looked better than before, as if whatever healing acceleration Fleet had done was continuing to work.

"You're ready to get this party started?" Jake asked.

"I'm beyond ready," Trent answered. "Looking forward to putting all this behind me."

"Good," I added, catching on to his double meaning, determined not to let him get to me. "Me too."

The four of us sat around the kitchen table. Fleet pointed at Trent. "The first thing we need to do is amp up your strength and increase your energy. Once we get you up to speed, we'll go to the Boardman."

"Whose collar will we remove?" I asked, suddenly remembering that with my mom dead, the only thing keeping me shielded now was this collar. "I know I'm the logical bait, but now that my dad and my mom are no longer alive, and with no one shielding me, this metal is the only thing keeping my aura from bursting like it did right before we time traveled."

"You know about your mom?" Fleet asked. "How?"

"I just do," I said, not wanting to get into my dreams.

"Aura bursting?" Jake asked.

"Yeah," I said. "My parents have been shielding me for so long that my aura will go berserk if set free, or something like that."

"I remember," Trent said.

"Your collar stays on then," Fleet said. "No matter what, and we'll deal with your energy explosion thing after we kill Farrell."

"I'll take my collar off," Trent offered.

"Nope," Fleet said. "I'll do it. I'm stronger right now." Not giving anyone time to object, he looked at Trent. "How long did it take Farrell to appear during our test run?"

"Nine seconds."

"That's not a lot of time," I said, my hands growing sweaty under the table. My anxiety over finally facing off against Farrell accelerated. Could we really kill him? Could I forget the old him and do what needed to be done?

Fleet shot me a reassuring look. "We don't need a lot of time. As soon as Farrell appears, we'll shoot him up with our power until—"

"He disintegrates," I said, finishing his sentence.

"Yes," Fleet said. "Exactly."

Tapping my foot under the table, I thought of what had happened to my dad, remembered the stream of energy that shot out of his mouth. We had found out later that the force had entered Farrell. "Where will Farrell's power go?"

"If we blast him into bits, it won't go anywhere," Jake answered.

"It'll just fade away?" Trent asked.

"That's right," Jake said. "I've seen it happen."

"Oh, okay, good," I said, clutching my knees under the table. The reality of what we were about to do weighed heavily on me. "Where will I be during all this?"

"You'll be with Trent," Fleet said. "He may not know what he's doing, but he's a Supreme, so he's the strongest one here."

"He's a what?" Jake asked. "Why didn't anyone tell me?"

Fleet shrugged. "It didn't seem important."

Jake scratched his head. "I guess not, and thinking back on what Trent can do, I should've known."

Trent looked uneasy being talked about as if he weren't there. "Okay, I've got Dominique. Fleet will take off his collar and then we shoot up Farrell when he appears. But what if...?" He paused, then asked bluntly, "What if it doesn't work?"

Fleet leaned forward in his chair. His hand on the table balled up into a fist. "Then we're all screwed."

***

We pushed the couch, chairs, and coffee table out of the way, creating a big, open space. Fleet positioned himself in the middle and waved Trent over.

"The first thing I need to do is charge you up," Fleet said.

Trent hesitated. "How?"

"It's like giving a car battery a jump." Fleet held out his arms, palms facing up. Trent placed his arms on top of Fleet's, gripping Fleet's forearms. "You ready?" Fleet asked.

Looking determined, Trent nodded.

The room stilled. Nobody breathed. An electrical buzz filled the air. Tendrils of smoky gray vapor came out of Fleet's hands and wrapped around Trent's. Moving like a current, the gray vapor travelled up and over Trent's arms.

Worried Trent was in pain, and afraid of something happening to him, I started to doubt Fleet's plan.

"He's going to be okay," Jake said, but his words didn't make me feel any better.

Trent's face turned red. His veins popped out of his neck. His body shook. Was it too much for him? I was steps away from rushing in and breaking their contact, when blue sparks discharged from Trent's hands. The flickering grew until a solid glow of sapphire radiated from Trent's skin, illuminating the entire room.

"Amazing," Jake said.

Covering my mouth with my hand as if to hold in my

amazement, I watched as Fleet's energy charged Trent's, multiplying it until Trent's aura shone almost as bright as a sun. Mesmerized by the phenomenon, I noticed a flicker of movement on Trent's face. Shielding my eyes, I saw Trent's burns and heat marks fade from bright red to his normal tan color. The bumps and scar tissue smoothed out.

"Holy crap, he's healing himself," Jake said.

The two Transhumans stayed locked in each other's grip, pulsing and pumping with energized particles. Trent's color grew bigger and brighter. Transfixed by the array, I noticed something weird about Fleet's cast. His glow dimmed. His output wavered. It was as if he were powering down because he was running out of juice.

"What's happening?" I muttered

"I don't know," Jake said.

Slowly rising off the floor, Trent towered over Fleet. Fleet's legs started to buckle. His arms trembled.

"Stop!" I called out. "Trent!"

Fleet started pulling away, but Trent wouldn't let him. He kept Fleet in a death grip, his own body looking like it might go supernova at any minute. Fleet tugged, grunting with effort. "Power down, man!" Fleet yelled.

Trent either couldn't hear, or couldn't stop himself. If he didn't let go, Fleet was the one who'd be obliterated. I clawed Jake's arm. "You have to separate them!"

Jake scanned the room, looking for a way to force Fleet and Trent apart. Finding nothing, Jake tucked his head down and barreled into Trent like a linebacker. Trent stumbled back, Fleet released his hold, and their deadly laser light show was extinguished.

Breathing heavy, Trent rubbed his head. "What happened?"

"You tried to kill me," Fleet said. "That's what the hell happened."

"I did?" Trent stared at his hands. "I'm really sorry," he said to Fleet. "I don't know what happened."

"It's like he's a live wire," Jake said. "Unpredictable and out of control."

A burst of flashing red and white light from outside the beach house streamed through the windows. Two loud siren blasts rang out. "The house is surrounded," a voice crackled over a megaphone. "We know you're in there, Hot Death. Come out with your hands on your head and no one will get hurt."

"Hot Death?" Trent asked out loud. "Who's that?"

"Me," Fleet grumbled, peeking out the blinds.

Jake, Trent, and I gathered behind Fleet and looked out the window, too. A small army of cop cars surrounded the lot. A helicopter flew overhead. A line of TV crews were parked out on the main street.

"Holy shit," Trent said. "What exactly do they think Hot Death did?"

"They think I kidnapped Infiniti. Now that she's been found at St. Joseph's, they probably think I killed her, too."

Panicked, I ordered, "We need to get out of here, now. We're too close to the end to let anything stop us."

"Dominique is right," Jake said. "Let's get out of here."

"You have two minutes to surrender before we come in!" The voice threatened.

"Get your stuff," Fleet commanded.

Jake popped into his room and reemerged with his pack slung over his shoulder. I remembered my pile of bloody clothes in the tub. "Hold on," I said. Rushing to the bathroom, I stared at my stained shirt and jeans for a minute, remorse over losing my best friend transfixing me.

"Hurry!" Trent called.

Pulled back to the urgency of the moment, I dug my

hand into my pants pocket and retrieved the Petoskey stone I had given Trent. Securing it in my new jeans, I slowly made my way out of there. My eyes lingered for a moment on the bed where Trent had told me he loved me, then scanned the floor where Jake and I had sat and watched over Trent while I he was healing.

"Now!" Jake urged.

Heavy boots thudded up the beach house stairs. My pulse skyrocketed. I dashed to the den and the others. They were standing in a circle, hands clasped. Taking a spot between Fleet and Trent, I linked fingers with them.

"Think of the Boardman," Fleet rushed out.

Misty gray, blue, and yellow vapor swirled around us. My legs started to feel wobbly. My body swayed. The door imploded with a kick. Cops in SWAT attire burst into view, and my friends and I slipped into a free fall.

Squeezing my eyes shut, ducking my head, and preparing for the worst, I realized I was standing on snow. Freezing temps hovered in the air. Clean air filtered into my lungs. "We made it," I said, finding it hard to believe we had transported out of the Galveston beach house without someone being shot or injured.

Jake smiled. "We did!" He released his grip and looked around, then said again, "We really did."

Infiniti had always believed in "signs." She was the ultimate optimist who saw the best in everything. Even at her death she told us not to be sad, and that she'd be back. Following her lead, I latched on to the success of the moment, seeing it as an indication that things were finally going our way. Maybe we could end this without any more of us getting hurt. Perhaps our plan to defeat Farrell would work. Eventually there had to be a change in tide.

This had to be it.

Chapter Twenty-Five

~ Trent ~

Dominique and Jake hugged and smiled, celebrating our safe escape from Galveston to Michigan, but I couldn't. In my mind, the worst lay ahead of us. We didn't have the luxury to let our guard down. At least, not yet.

"I wouldn't throw a party just yet," Fleet admonished, taking in our surroundings.

With my body shivering from the drastic drop in temperature, I scanned the area too. Not far in the distance I spotted the roof of the cabin. But with the fire damage inside, we couldn't go there. "Where to?" I asked.

Fleet started walking away in the opposite direction of the log house. "Richard and Sue have a bunk house down the way. Come on."

Boots crunching on the snowy ground, we trudged down a path until a long and narrow, wooden and rustic-looking structure sprang into view. We entered through the unlocked, sliding glass door. The frigid draft inside penetrated my jeans and shirt, cutting into my bones with icy stealth.

Dominique's teeth chattered. "It's c-c-colder in here than outside," she said, every word puffing out of her mouth in a cloudy vapor. She hugged herself. "P-please tell me this place has a heat."

"It does," Jake said. "A furnace." He pointed to a door at the back of the room. "Over there."

Jake and Fleet went to inspect our source of warmth, and I moved closer to Dominique. Putting my arms around her, I drew her in and rubbed her back.

"Thanks, T-T-Trent," she chattered.

A low rumble shook the walls, and the smell of burning oil seeped through the room. "Thank goodness," she whispered, still staying close to me as her body shook. "I wonder how long it'll t-t-take for this place to get warm."

"Hopefully not too long," I answered, holding her a little closer.

Fleet and Jake rejoined us. Wasting no time getting back on track, Jake said, "We're here. We know what to do. Are we ready to do this thing?"

"I'm ready," Fleet said. "If everyone else is."

"Let's warm up a little first," I suggested. "Maybe find some sweatshirts or something." We were all wearing jeans and long sleeves, but if we were going to be outside, we needed more clothes.

"Good idea," Dominique said, her body relaxing a tad as warmth started filling the room.

"Come on, then," Fleet said, leading us up narrow, rickety stairs at the far side of the room. "There's stuff to wear up here."

Twin-sized beds lined one side of the second floor of the bunk house, reminding me of a fairy tale room. Closets lined the other. Digging around, we found tons of sweatshirts.

"Why do Richard and Sue have all these beds and clothes?" I asked, finding a navy, fleece sweatshirt and pulling it on.

Fleet hung back, not interested in adding to his wardrobe. "This place has been a refuge for our kind forever. Before our numbers diminished, Pures passed through here all the time. Richard and Sue welcomed every last visitor. They even hosted a massive Thanksgiving dinner every year. People came from all over the world."

Jake laughed. "It was the best meal you'd ever eaten. Multiple turkeys, hams, side dishes galore." He found a dark, red sweater and pulled it over his head. "And the pies. Mmm. Most scrumptious pies on the planet."

Dominique had slipped on a white sweatshirt. Pulling off her boots, she started layering on socks. "I wish I remembered them. Uncle Richard and Aunt Sue." She cast her eyes down. "I wish I remembered a lot of things. Our fates might have turned out differently for us if I had."

Fleet leaned against the wall and ran his fingers through his hair. "It doesn't matter now."

"I guess not," she muttered.

Adrift in my own thoughts, I started thinking about the people we'd lost. Above all, Infiniti. Her lifeless eyes, the blood pouring out of her body. If only I could've done something to help her. Then I thought of Abuela, probably worried sick back home. I said a little prayer in my head for her, hoping she was okay.

"Trent?" Pulled back to reality, I saw Dominique in front of me, her hand on my shoulder. The others going back down the stairs.

"Sorry," I said to her, giving my head a little shake. "No emotions. I got it. You don't have to tell me."

Her mouth parted, her lips trembled. Did she want to kiss me? One last time? I waited for her to make a move, but all she did was back up. "That's right. No emotions. Come on."

Back downstairs with the room almost completely warm, we decided not to put off the inevitable.

"Are we going to the fire pit again?" I asked Fleet.

"Yes."

"We get in a circle and then you take off your collar, right?" Dominique asked Fleet.

Fleet held up the plastic file. "That's right."

"You should get in the middle of the circle, Dominique, so we can form a defensive band around you," I said.

"But stay closest to Trent," Fleet said. "And Trent, you keep your thoughts on protecting the Marked One. It will help focus your energy."

"Good idea," Dominique said.

"As soon as Farrell shows, we light him up like the fourth of July," Fleet said. "No hesitation."

"No hesitation," Jake repeated.

"None," I agreed.

We studied each other, waiting for someone to say something else, but no one did. Thinking of Roland, Matthew, and Huxley, and how I had huddled with them before going into the church, I stuck out my hand. "Infiniti on three."

Dominique placed her hand on mine, followed by Jake, and then Fleet. "One, two, three, Infiniti," we chanted.

Our voices echoed in the bunk house for a minute before we made our way to the circular clearing where Richard and Sue had set up their fire pit. The sun had moved across the March sky, almost touching the Western horizon. The heavens were painted with splashes of pink, orange, and red. I couldn't help but think that if this were it for me, it certainly was a glorious day. And I had definitely lived a good life.

Don't think that way.

I looked over my shoulder, expecting to find Abigail, but my gaze only met a snowy landscape.

"What is it, Trent?" Dominique whispered to me, looking in the same direction.

"It's nothing," I answered.

Fleet, Jake, and I surrounded Dominique. Her pale face displayed an emotion I hadn't seen before on her—readiness. Her stance was wide, her gaze fierce. She inched closer to me. "I'm ready."

"Let's do this," Fleet said. He held the plastic file up to the collar around his throat. Stretching his neck to one side, he poked the thin, rubbery, material between his skin and the metal. His teeth gritted as he swiped it around. "Almost there," he said. "Hold on."

A snap sounded. The collar fell off. I started counting. "One, two, three, four—"

An explosion shook the Earth. The ground split beneath our feet. I lunged for Dominique, but she slipped out of view, plunging into the crevice below her.

Chapter Twenty-Six

~ Dominique ~

Standing in the circle facing Trent, I forced myself not to feel anything for him. Even though I desperately wanted to go to him, tell him how much he meant to me, I stayed in my place. Cold air bit at my face. Nerves wrestled my gut. Fear held me in a grip. "No emotions," I repeated to myself.

Fleet poked the plastic device between his skin and the collar. A click sounded. The choker thudded to the ground. Trent started counting.

No emotions, no emotions, no emotions.

The idea of killing Farrell seemed less possible with each number that spilled out of Trent's mouth. Out of nowhere, a tingle of panic raced across my spine. And then, an eerie stillness surrounded me. The winds stopped blowing. The wildlife silenced. When Trent reached the four-second count, a rumble shook the earth. The ground beneath my feet tore open. Trent yelled my name. He stretched out his hand, but it was too late. My body dropped into nothingness.

***

"They have no idea what I can do," Farrell said.

Opening my eyes, I found myself lying on the shore of my favorite beach. Gritty sand pressed against my cheek. The scents of dirt and lake water filled my nose. Raising myself up on my forearms, I saw Farrell. He sat on a cluster of rocks, staring at me.

The sun had started to set, washing the sky in pastel hues, exactly like the sky I had just left at the Boardman. But where were the others?

"They're not coming," Farrell said. He rose to his feet, held out his hand, and helped me to mine.

"Is this real?" I asked, looking around for Mom, Dad, Jan, Abigail, and Infiniti, but not finding them. This time it was just him and me. "Am I really here? Or is this another dream?"

"Another dream? So you've been dreaming of me?" he asked, wiping granules of pebbles from my face.

"Yes, and you told me to…" I stopped, realizing the version of him in my dreams had to have been my mind reaching out for the old Farrell, the Farrell I had fallen for who no longer existed. That Farrell would rather die than hurt me.

"It doesn't matter what you manifested in your dreams. This is real, and this is the end for you, Dominique. Nothing can change that now."

He cupped my face in his strong hands, looking down on me with deep hazel eyes that used to be pure green but weren't anymore after his change. He pulled me in and hugged me. "Are you ready?"

Taking in a series of shallow breaths, my heart raced at the thought of dying for the last and final time. A sense of impending doom and closure lay heavy on me. He had to die, but with the others gone, I had no idea what to do.

Farrell's gaze roamed every inch of my face. "I am so in love with you, Dominique. With every shred of who I am. And I wish I didn't have to do this."

Pressure built in my chest, slowly but inevitably, until it consumed my heart, sending waves of pain, regret, and remorse pulsing through my very soul. As I sank into despair, and at my lowest moment, the image of one person sprang to mind—Trent. In a normal world, we would've dated, gone to prom, separated for college, yet kept in touch because neither one of us could forget or replace the other. Over time, we would've started dating again, married, and maybe even had kids. But this wasn't a normal world. I wasn't an ordinary girl. And I wondered if I should have chosen him this life.

"You don't love me anymore, do you?" Farrell asked. I did love him, but not like this. He must've seen the truth on my face. Maybe even felt it on a spiritual level. He furrowed his brow, and hurt sprang to his yes. "Do you?"

"No, I mean, yes… I mean, why does it matter!" I charged him and pounded my fists against his chest. "Just do it already! Kill me!"

I will be so pissed if you give up that easily.

Drawing in a sharp breath, I searched the shore for Infiniti. Had I really heard her? Or was my mind playing tricks on me again?

Farrell followed my line of sight. "What are you looking for?"

"Nothing," I said, fixing a hard glare on him, suddenly knowing that I couldn't let down Infiniti or the others. Breathing heavy, my pulse racing and my blood pumping, my brain scrambled to figure out a way to fight back, but I couldn't think of anything.

Then I thought that I could at least try to save the

others. "If I let you have me without a fight, will you let the others live?"

Shouting drifted my way. The words "fight," "no," and "don't" meeting my ears. Peering about I spotted my cheering squad in the distance—Mom, Dad, Infiniti, Jan, and Abigail. Their pleas made me regret my offer, but I waited for Farrell's response anyway.

Biting the inside of my cheek, I stared at Farrell, wondering if he heard their cries, but he gave no indication. Finally, he answered me. "No. Everyone must die."

He brought his hands to my face, stroked my cheeks for a minute, and then worked his grip down to the collar I still wore. "This device can't save you. Nothing can now."

An idea clicked in my brain. The device. The metal. With my parents dead, it was the only thing keeping my aura muffled. Maybe if I separated it from my skin, I could fight Farrell with my light. But then I remembered I had no plastic device to snap it off.

Farrell ran his hands down my neck. "They say people know everything once they die. That all the secrets of the universe will be revealed. I'm hoping it'll be that way for you. In death, you'll finally see that I'm doing this for you, Dominique. To save you."

"No, you're not," I choked out.

Ignoring my words, he secured one hand behind my neck and held me still. He hovered his other hand over my heart. "I'll do my best to make this quick and painless."

Tensing my body, my gut twisting into a tight knot, I readied myself for the blow.

"And now," Farrell said. "I take your life force."

Those words. They were the same ones Tavion had used in the red desert. Reeling from the irony of my fate, hating Tavion for still playing a role in my destiny, Farrell plunged his hand into my chest. A jolt of electricity shot into me, my body stiffened. My legs shook.

Fight! Right the hell now!

Okay! I yelled to Infiniti in my head.

Gasping for air, my body writhing in pain, I clawed at my collar, trying to wrestle it off. The torque tightened from my effort. The metal points lining the inside of the choker bore into my skin. My brain zapped with pain. I didn't know which was worse, the fiery blast Farrell unleashed into my body, or the stabbing cuts probing into my neck and throat.

Hurry, Mom and Dad said.

Before it's too late, my dear, Jan added.

Kick his ass! Infiniti demanded.

I forced my fingers between my skin and the metal. Digging my digits around, slippery with what had to have been my own blood, the tip of my fingernail made contact with a raised button. My index finger inched over the nub. Grunting with effort and struggling for breath, I pressed, trying to separate the shard from my skin, but every move I made only amplified my pain. My vision started to fade my muscles weakening.

"Stop," I gurgled, gazing into Farrell's face, a face I used to love. "Please."

His eyes blazed with glowing flecks of white and gold. His face grimaced in wicked determination. No matter what had happened to him, no matter what he had said, I knew this wasn't him. There was no way. And even though I didn't want to hurt him, I had to.

Making one last attempt and growling with effort, I channeled all my strength to my hand. My fingers stretched. My muscles pushed. Getting a firm position over the button, I pressed with all my force. The pointer inside the collar depressed, pulling out of my skin. The deadly necklace tumbled to the ground.

Farrell released his hold from the back of my neck, as if losing the metal had somehow jarred him. His energy blast barreling into my chest wavered, and he stumbled back. My legs buckled and I crashed to the pebbly ground. Shocked that I had managed to remove the device, and waiting for my light to shoot out of me before he attacked again, I caught sight of a white feather half-buried in the sand. My symbol of hope. I scooped it up with my crimson stained hand, and held it to my chest. Thoughts of my love for Farrell, the old him, filled me, and a soft humming came from my body.

"You told me not to have emotions," I said to Farrell. "In my dream. But I can't help it."

He came at me with renewed determination. "You have to die. It's the only way."

No, you don't, my loved ones said, now surrounding me. I held out my hand, and they joined me, lifting theirs in solidarity. Calling on my love for those who had died for me, and focusing on what I had with Farrell, I concentrated on my aura. Inner strength coursed through my veins, the veil from my true self lifted, and a soft light came out of skin. Suddenly I felt like I could do anything.

"No," I said to Farrell. He stopped in his tracks, as if he had run into an invisible wall.

A tingling vibration spread over my skin. My face flushed. My lips trembled. A multi-colored stream of soothing vapor poured out of me. The hue circled Farrell's boots. Like a slow moving fog, it crawled up his body, covering every last inch of him. It grew bigger and brighter with each passing second, pulsing and tightening around him.

He jerked his body back and forth. "You have to die, Marked One! You have to!"

"*Don't listen to him,*" Infiniti said, her shimmery body standing between me and Farrell. "*Farrell will never be the same, and because of that, he's not part of your destiny anymore.*" She squeezed my hand. "*You have to end him now or eventually he'll end you and every last Pure.*"

She opened my hand, took away the feather I still gripped, and replaced it with Trent's Petoskey stone. "*I think I died so I could help you focus on what you have before you.*" She tapped the stone.

Infiniti faded away. My stare locked on the fossilized rock. The coral impressions on it pulsed blue. I knew Trent's energy had been absorbed into the object. I knew it could help me.

"Don't do this, Dominique!" Farrell pleaded, still squirming and trying to escape from the circular force field that held him tight.

"I'm sorry, Farrell," I said, knowing the Farrell from my dreams had been warning me to bottle my feelings for him so I could do what needed to be done in this very moment. "The real you wants me to live. And so do I."

Hot tears stung my eyes and my heart filled with pain. Forcing myself to ignore my feelings, I concentrated on love and light, wishing Farrell a peaceful end.

A deafening buzz filled the air. Blue wisps of power from the stone mixed with my multi-colored light. The current holding Farrell pulsed bright, amplifying until it burst into a shower of sparks. My body flew back from the explosion. Heat sprayed my face. Climbing back up to my feet, I saw Farrell was gone. Nothing of him remained. He had disintegrated just like in my dreams.

I dropped back down to my knees as if I had just run

a marathon, and let my rapid breathing slowly return to normal. I glanced around for Infiniti and the others but didn't find them.

"It's done," I said out loud.

Now that I had survived, all I had to do was get back to the others. But how? Scanning Elk Rapids beach, hoping to find someone to help me, I thought of the Petoskey stone I still held. I squeezed it tight.

Trent, I need you.

Chapter Twenty-Seven

~ Trent ~

Diving forward, arm outstretched, I caught sight of Dominique's terror-filled eyes before she slipped from view. The ripped earth closed up behind her. I face-planted on the ground where she had stood, and pounded at the surface. "Dominique!"

Fleet and Jake were on their hands and knees beside me, digging at the earth, hollering for Dominique, too.

Fleet pushed to his feet. "Shoot it up!"

Barely giving Jake and me enough time to get out of the way, Fleet discharged everything he had at the spot. Jake joined him and together they pummeled the turf with surges of energy-filled rage. Staring dumbfounded at the landscape, puffs of plume-filled haze clouding the area, I knew our efforts were futile.

"She's gone," I whispered.

Jake sank to his knees, and eventually, so did Fleet. Shock held us in place as if we had been zapped by a stun gun. Jake kept a steady gaze on the ground. "The only way we can reach her is if her collar is removed."

"That's right," I muttered, a sliver of hope sparking inside of me. "Then we can track her signature."

"Yes," Jake said. "Theoretically."

Fleet paced like a wild animal. "How can that happen though? Removing the collar? She doesn't have the plastic file."

"She'll find a way," I said.

"All we can do is wait," Jake added. "And hope that somehow she can do it."

Antsy and on edge, we waited for any sign of Dominique. We combed the area for clues, and even called out to her as if she could hear us. Seconds turned to minutes, the minutes turned to hours, and the day turned to night. Fleet erected two bonfires, one on either side of the spot where Dominique had vanished, bathing the area in a fiery, red glow.

I was almost ready to give up hope, believing we had lost Dominique forever, when a strange sensation came over me. I stilled myself, trying to decipher the feelings building inside of me, when I recognized love. Affection. Even a touch of homesickness. It filled my heart, and I knew right away it was Dominique.

"I can feel her," I said in a low voice, not wanting the sensation to go away.

Fleet stomped over to me. He latched on to my arm. "Let me see."

His hand warmed. His gray power manifested. Instead of oozing out and wrapping around me, it pulsed like a drum. "It's her," he said.

"It is?" Jake asked, excited and hopeful. "Hurry! Get her, before it's too late."

"On it," Fleet muttered.

Keeping his hand on me, he closed his eyes. He pointed his other hand at the place where Dominique vanished. His aura channeled out of him. It poured out onto the snowy ground, shrouding the area in a gray fog. "Come on, dammit," he said.

Willing her to appear, desperate to see her, roaring blue energy screamed out of me. It mixed with Fleet's and took over, washing the scene in cobalt brilliance.

"Ease up," Fleet gritted.

His warning whispered at me like a nagging tickle at the back of my mind, but I couldn't comply because I didn't know how. My instincts had taken over. My desire to save Dominique pushed the sapphire beams out of me.

"It's working!" Jake called out.

The outline of a body formed amidst the energy field. Faint at first, it continued to solidify until Dominique fully appeared. Blood covered one of her hands. A dark purple bruise circled her throat where her collar had been. Blood trickled from one side of her neck and trailed down her shirt. She staggered to the ground.

"I got her," Jake said, swooping in. "I need to stop her bleeding." He zipped open his backpack and started rifling through his things.

Fleet released his hold and eyed me. "You need to learn to control that," he warned.

He was right. I had no command over what I could do, but I didn't care. All that mattered was getting Dominique back in one piece. But where was Farrell?

Fleet scanned our surroundings, obviously thinking the same thing. "Where the hell is he?"

A supersonic shrill pierced my ears, the tone so strong I thought my ear drums would burst. Doubling over on the ground, I slammed my hands over my head. The pain partially blinded my sight. Stars danced before my eyes. My head felt as if a hammer battered against it. Not far away I spotted Fleet on the ground, too.

"You dumb asses," Jake yelled over the din. Carrying a small, black box in his hand, he kicked Fleet in the gut. "Stupid, dumb, assholes."

"What the hell are you doing!" Fleet hollered, doubled over with agony and covering his ears like me.

"You'll find out," Jake said. Sauntering over to me, he kicked me in the side right where I had been shot. A yell burst out of me. Agonizing spasms rippled through my body. He manipulated the box, pushing a button on it. The choker around my neck dug into my skin like a thousand little daggers.

After a few seconds, the pain subsided enough for me to steady my gaze. I frantically searched for Dominique and saw her just as she jumped on Jake's back. With a quick maneuver, he flung her off and blasted a stream of yellow at her chest, sending her crashing into a tree. She fell to the ground in a heap.

"No!" I yelled, clambering to my feet.

Jake touched a dial on the box. The shrill softened, yet the burn in my ears and head intensified. The spines on the inside of the collar gouged deeper into my flesh. Jake swiped my feet out from under me with a kick, levelling me in an instant.

"Have you dumb asses figured it out yet that you have no power? That you're defenseless?"

What? I concentrated on my aura, trying to shoot it out of me, but nothing happened.

Jake circled me and Fleet. "I told you."

He showered a spray of vapor over me and wrapped me in a cocoon of energized webbing. He did the same to Fleet. "You see this little invention of mine?" He bent down and waved the black box in front of my face, then lifted it for Fleet to see. "With that device around your neck, and with this controller in my hand, I own you." He took off his own collar and flung it on the ground. "Like dogs."

Pain from the choker continued shooting into my skin. My ears throbbed from the signal seeping up through ear canal and into my brain. Trying to block it out, I concentrated on my light again, commanding it to unleash, but it wouldn't. Thrashing about, I found the web that wrapped around me impenetrable.

"You're so dead," I threatened.

"No, you are. And then Fleet. But first, I need to kill Dominique. Once and for all."

Jake marched over to Dominique. Her body lay motionless on the ground. Angry enough to kill Jake with my bare hands, I peered at Fleet. "We have to do something," I said to him.

"I know." He tried to kick his legs, but couldn't move them. He even bit at the live netting that wrapped his body to no avail.

"I have an idea," I said. "Scoot over to me."

I started inching closer to him, and he did the same. All the while, I kept one eye on Dominique. She sat up, her hands balled into fists on her lap. Jake leaned in, talking to her in a low voice. With each word, the look on her face rotated from surprise, to hurt, to anger. I had no idea what he was saying to her, but I knew it wasn't good.

I also knew that Fleet and I were her only hope for survival.

Chapter Twenty-Eight

~ Dominique ~

My head pounded, my brain rattled, and I didn't know where I was.

"Hey, wake up," a voice said. "Can you hear me? Dominique, it's me."

Who?

I pressed my hands to my forehead, then rubbed my eyes. Coming out of my haze, I saw Jake crouching down in front of me. Jake… Jake! He had attacked Trent and Fleet and blasted me against a tree! I tried to spring to my feet, but my legs were too shaky.

"What the hell, Jake?" I inched away from him, my palms scraping against the snow, but I didn't get far. My back met a hard surface, and I cried out with pain

"Oh no," he said sarcastically. "Are you hurt?"

Every inch of my body ached, from my bruised backside to the burning pain at my neck, down to the throbbing of my blood soaked fingers.

"You're a mess," Jake said.

Peering around him, I saw Trent and Fleet. There were immobilized on the floor, both of them secured in a web of Jake's electrical power. But what the hell was happening? Why did Jake attack them?

"What's going on?" I asked in a terror-laced voice. Then I spied a black remote control looking device in his hand. "What's that?"

He held it up. "Oh this? I call it my veil commander. It's connected to the collars and it gives me complete control over the wearer. Since you're not wearing yours anymore, you can't hear the shrill your friends are hearing right now or feel the pain coursing through their bodies." He pushed a button, and Trent and Fleet seized, as if someone poked them with a hot stick.

I made a fist and slammed it against his face. "Stop!"

He smirked, then rubbed his cheek. "Okay, I'll stop. For now." He released the button on the black box and eyed me. "There's a lot I want to tell you anyway, so let's get started."

The flaming tongues of the bonfire roared behind Jake, casting a devilish glow in the background. Had he been working against me this whole time? If he had, how did we not know?

"I see the wheels turning in your brain," he said. "And I promise, before your final death, you'll understand everything."

After defeating Tavion, expunging the evil within me with the help of Trent's ancestors, and saying good-bye to Farrell, now I had to face Jake. My best friend from first life. None of it made sense. But then I realized something. Every single time I had been at death's door, Trent had saved me. Back at the red desert, he had touched my cross that released Abigail's energy that brought me back from the dead. In 1930, his great-grandmother cleansed me with an ancient Hispanic ritual. And then, with Farrell, it was the Petoskey stone that helped me defeat him that later allowed Trent and Fleet locate me. The stone. I palmed it in my hand behind my back. Maybe I could call on it again.

Jake moved up close to my face. "What are you thinking about in that pretty little head of yours?"

"I'm wondering why you're doing this. Why you turned on me."

As if settling in for a bedtime story, he sat back and said, "Do you remember how I told you about Olivia, and how I had fallen in love with her?"

"Yes."

"Well, when she died, I died. A huge piece of me anyway. I didn't want to live without her, couldn't stand not seeing her every day. Touching her. Kissing her. Being with her. I didn't think I'd recover from her loss, but after a few decades, I met another amazing girl. I didn't want to fall in love, had no intention of feeling that kind of pain again, but I couldn't help it. It just happened. I fell for her, hard, and she for me. And it was Olivia all over again."

His face contorted by the memory of her loss. My heart hurt for him, and I wished I could do something for him... besides dying.

"Do you know what that's like, Dominique? To suffer such loss? Do you have any idea?"

I wanted to say yes, but knew whatever I said would be the wrong response so I didn't answer. Instead, I said, "I'm sorry about everything you've been through, Jake. I really am. But what does all this have to do with me?"

Jake kicked at a mound of snow. The fire behind him sizzled and popped. "Everything."

Trying to be inconspicuous, I leaned slightly to the side to catch a glimpse of Trent and Fleet. They were still netted, their collars still on, and their power still disabled. But then I noticed a slight movement. The two of them were slowly inching toward each other. They had to have a plan for our escape. If so, they'd need time, which meant Jake had to keep talking. "Can you please tell me?"

Jake slammed down the buttons of his handheld device, sending Trent and Fleet's bodies into agony. Then he got up and walked their way.

"Please, leave them alone," I said to myself.

"I'll tell you everything," he said. "After I fix the fire." Stepping over Trent and Fleet, ignoring them as if they were inanimate objects, Jake rekindled the fire. I didn't even realize how cold I was until new warmth washed over me. It was as if I had become numbed to the frigid air.

Jake came back and sat down in front of me. He took a deep breath. "You need to die because the entire race needs to die. I *want* it to die. I *need* it to die. No one should have to endure what I've endured." He pounded his fist on the earth. "No one!"

He waited for me to say something, but I had no words.

"Do you remember when we talked about the prophecy?"

I remembered our plunge into the ocean, the note he drew out of his pocket in my handwriting telling me to kill Farrell, and the exact words of the prophecy. I muttered them out loud, "First will be the changing that comes from within. Second will be the changing that comes from without. Third will be the demise of those linked to the One."

He pounded his chest. "I'm the change from without. Get it? You thought the prophecy meant being without your protectors, but it was talking about me!"

"What?" Shivers of ice cold ran down my spine. "You?"

"Yes! Because I left after first life. You were without ME!" Rage laced his words. Hate spewed from his eyes. "And that note to kill Farrell? I wrote it! I needed you to kill him and get him out of the way because if I killed you first, I knew he'd come after me!"

"I didn't write that note?"

"After all this time, copying your handwriting was a piece of cake. Do you want to know why it was so easy?" On his feet now, he towered over me, like a possessed demon. His body shook with rage. "Ask me why!"

"Why!" I hollered back, trying to scoot away from him but unable to with the trees behind me.

He reached his hand up in his shirt, yanked at something, and pulled out a necklace with a dark charm. He swung it in front of my face. "I believe you lost this on the plane."

My body shivered. I pressed a fisted hand to my mouth. It was my bloodstone cross, the cross that Trent's grandmother had given me. The last time I had it on was when Fleet, Farrell, and I flew from Elk Rapids to Houston. When I got off the plane, I realized I wasn't wearing it anymore.

I reached up to snatch it away, but Jake pulled it back and slipped it over his head. "I don't think so."

"You were there? On the plane?" I asked, stunned and sick to my stomach.

He leaned toward me. "I've been everywhere. Watching. Studying. Waiting. Plotting."

Movement behind Jake caught my eye. Sparks of gray and blue flickered. Puffs of energized vapor drifted up into the cold air. Were Trent and Fleet getting free? I had to keep Jake focused on me. I had to do whatever I could to give them more time.

Eyeing the black box in his hand, but careful not to let my gaze stay on it too long, I knew I needed it so I could free my friends. "You've been watching me this whole time?" I crossed my arms. "I don't believe you." Tucking the Petoskey stone in my back pocket, I readied myself to lunge for the device.

Enraged, Jake recited major milestones in my life like gathering stones with my dad at Dock Road, moving to Houston, going to Infiniti's, meeting Trent. He went on while particles of energy from Trent and Fleet drifted behind him. But then, like a switch being flipped, he stopped. He sniffed the air. He was about to turn around when I leapt to my feet and tackled him to the ground. I clawed his face, digging my nails into his skin, and grappled for the controller. It slid away and out of reach.

"Dominique!" Trent called out. "Catch!"

Halfway out of his Transhuman trap, Trent tossed one of the collars my way. Kneeing Jake in the groin, I caught the metal choker and snapped it around Jake's neck. Scooping up the black remote from a pile of snow, I clambered to my feet and started pushing the buttons.

"You asshole," I said. His body squirmed. His neck started to burn. Thick, dark foam billowed out of his mouth. "*You* are the final death!" I yelled, going crazy on the device, slamming on the controls like a mad person until Jake exploded into a million little pieces of dust.

Stumbling back away from the spot where Jake had blown up, I sank to my knees. Dust landed on my hands and face, sprinkling over me like Armageddon.

Trent approached me with caution. "Hey," he said. He slipped the device from my grasp. He put his hands on my shoulders. "It's over."

Fleet came up behind Trent, worry on his face. "You okay?"

"Yes," I muttered, trying to sound like I meant it, but then changed my answer. "No."

Everything was over. We had won.

But nothing would ever be okay.

Chapter Twenty-Nine

~ Trent ~

Scooping Dominique up in my arms, I carried her to the bunkhouse. Silent and still, devoid of emotion, she curled up in my arms. Halfway there, I heard soft whimpering sounds coming from her.

"Shh," I said, holding her closer to me. "It's going to be okay. I got you now."

Once inside, I took her upstairs and placed her on one of the beds. Dried blood and bruises riddled her neck. Her face was so pale she could pass for a dead person. I stroked her cheek. "Let me see if I can find something for your cuts."

She sat up with a start and grabbed my sleeve. "Don't leave me. Please."

I put my hand on top of hers and squeezed. "I'll be right back. I promise."

She stayed upright, the look in her eyes telling me she didn't believe me. "Where's Fleet?"

"He stayed back by the bonfire, clearing the scene. He'll be here in a minute."

She slowly lowered herself back on the bed. "Okay."

Scouring the closets and the bathrooms, I finally

found a first aid kit tucked inside a cabinet in the kitchenette downstairs. Going back up to Dominique, I found her in the exact same position as I left her, frozen in grief and pain.

"I'm back," I said, sitting on the edge of the bed. I opened the box and started taking things out. Band-Aids, gauze, ointments, wipes, and even some ibuprofen—the kit had everything Dominique needed.

Eyeing her to make sure she wasn't in shock, but not really sure how to tell, I peeled open three packets of alcohol wipes. I folded the wet pads between my fingers. "This might sting a little." She was still quiet. I blotted her neck, wiping away as much blood as I could. Then I went to work on her fingers, rubbing as gently as possible. "That doesn't hurt, does it?"

Still no reaction.

With most of the blood cleaned off, I tore open the ointment. Squiring it onto my fingertips, I smoothed the salve over her cuts. "This should feel good," I said. The steady rise and fall of her chest was the only thing that told me she was still alive. "You're freaking me out a little," I said with a laugh, trying not to alarm her, but also hoping to stir life into her. I moved my face closer to hers. "Are you in there? Can you hear me?"

Her lips stuck together, but slowly parted. "Yes."

"Good." With her wounds covered with the glossy cream, I unraveled the gauze. "I'm going to lift your head and wrap your neck, okay?"

She nodded ever so slightly.

Eyeing the purple and black bruises on her skin, and the gashes where the collar had been, I gently lifted her head and started covering her injuries. Fresh anger over what had happened to her flooded my mind, but I didn't let it show. Dominique needed me to keep my cool.

"Now the hand," I said. I bandaged it up first, then secured the dressings with the gauze. I placed her hand back down on the bed. "There," I said. "All done."

The bottom door of the bunkhouse creaked open and slammed shut. "It's just me," Fleet called out.

His boots pounded across the downstairs floor, and then up the stairs. He came next to Dominique. He took a good look at her, and I could see the worry in his eyes. "She alright?"

"Yeah, she's good. Everything cleaned up by the bonfire?"

Fleet leaned against the wall. "Yeah. There's no trace of anyone or anything." He held up Dominique's necklace with the bloodstone cross. "I was able to recover this."

"My cross," she said. I tried not to be jealous that Fleet had gotten her to speak.

"Here," Fleet said.

He bent down and slipped it over her neck. Her hand trembled as she gripped the stone. "Thanks, Fleet."

My exhaustion was catching up to me. I sat on the floor next to Dominique's bed. Fleet joined me. He ran his fingers through his hair. "Now what?"

My eyes hurt, my ears throbbed, and my bones were fatigued. I shook my head, almost not believing everything that had happened. "We go back home. Make up an excuse about where we've been and what happened. Try to return to our normal lives."

"I don't do normal," Fleet said. "Plus, I'm wanted. Hot Death. Remember?"

Of course I remembered, but I didn't know what to say. "What will you do?"

"What I always do. Get away, stay underground, mind my own damned business. Disappear forever. Nobody will ever see Hot Death again."

The soft rattle from the furnace shook the walls. Gusts of wind outside brushed up against the house. A sinking feeling settled into my gut, as if there was no way to ever be normal again.

Dominique shifted in her bed, swung her legs over the side, and slid down onto the floor with us. "You're leaving?" she asked Fleet, her face full of sorrow and regret.

"I have to."

She leaned her head on his shoulder, but didn't say anything.

"What about you and Dominique?" Fleet asked me. "How can you explain Dominique's survival after her staged car crash? The authorities think she, her parents, and Farrell were killed in that accident."

Joining the conversation, Dominique said, "I can say that I wasn't in the car at the time of the crash." She stopped to consider her tale. "That losing my parents pushed me over the edge and I fell into a deep depression."

"And your injuries?" Fleet asked.

She looked up and away, as if searching for a good lie. "I can say a man kidnapped me while I was hitchhiking and attacked me, and that I eventually got away."

I considered her story. "I think everyone will buy that," I said.

"And you?" Fleet asked me.

I leaned my head against the wall and stared up at the wood-beamed ceiling, trying to come up with something believable. "I can say that I went looking for Dominique after her car crash because I didn't believe she had actually died."

"I know," Dominique added. "I can say I called you after I escaped and you came for me."

"Yeah," I said. "That'll work."

As another lull of silence fell down on us, nervousness over rejoining society set in, and my gut clenched.

"Do you think we can ever put this behind us?" Dominique asked.

"I don't know," I said.

"I want to put it behind me," she said. "I want to forget everything we've been through and start over with my life. My last life."

"I hear you," Fleet said.

The three of us sat in silence, thinking of our stories, mulling them over in our brains to make sure they were airtight and made sense. And then we agreed to stay the night in the bunkhouse and get rest. Throwing an armful of blankets and pillows on the ground, the three of us slept together on the floor, bound by tragedy, joined by survival.

Dominique's desire to start over rang loudly in my head until I finally fell asleep.

***

The next morning, Fleet was gone. No note, no mushy good-byes, just a quiet disappearance.

Bundled up in jackets, hats and gloves, Dominique and I set out on foot for the main road. It didn't take long for us to flag down a car and recount our tale. The driver, a nice old lady who referred to herself as Aunt Yokey, raced us to the hospital.

Once in, we were swarmed by hospital staff. Cops arrived, and later the FBI. Separated from Dominique, I wondered if she was okay. I worried about her state of mind.

After three days of isolation, we were both released. Me to my grandmother, and Dominique to Infiniti's mom.

Dominique hardly looked at me in the cab as we drove to the airport. She even kept her distance on the plane. I wondered what was going through her head, though I already knew. She was starting over and putting me behind her.

Finally home, I crashed down on my bed and lay perfectly still. Forcing myself to breathe slowly, trying to find some sort of peace within me, I suddenly knew what I needed to do. I needed to start over, too.

"Mijo," Abuela said in a half-whisper at my door. "Are you okay? I'm worried about you." She sat at the edge of my bed and rubbed my leg. "You've been through a lot."

"I'll be okay," I said, but not exactly believing it.

She gave my leg one last pat and got up to leave my room. Pausing at the door, she said, *"No dejes para mañana lo que puedas hacer hoy."*

I raised my head and watched her disappear from view, her words echoing in my head. *Don't wait for tomorrow to do something you can do today.*

Dashing out to my car, I headed straight for Infiniti's house and Dominique. I parked in front of the two-story brick structure. Gathering my courage, I approached the home slowly, wondering if I was doing the right thing. With a gift bag in hand, I rang the bell. Dominique opened the door.

"Hi, are you Dominique?"

She tilted her head and gave me a curious look.

"I'm Trent and I heard you were new to Houston. I wanted to come by and introduce myself and give you a welcome-to-the-neighborhood gift." I handed her the bag.

She stared at it for a few seconds before taking out the tissue paper and pulling out a snow globe, the same globe I had given her at Christmas that she had left in her house before she and her parents left. Her eyes welled up with tears.

"I heard you were from Michigan and that snowy little town in that globe reminded me of up north. I hope you like it."

She held it to her chest. "Thank you. I love it. It's perfect." She opened the door. "Would you like to come in?"

"Sure," I said, stepping into the house, thinking maybe we could start over.

Together.

THE END

Note from the Author:

Thank you so much for taking the time to read *Final Death*! If you enjoyed the story, I would appreciate it if you would help others enjoy this book, too.

Lend it. This e-book is lending enabled, so please share it with a friend.

Recommend it. Please tell other readers why you liked this book by reviewing it at your favorite e-retailer and/or review site.

Review it. Please tell other readers why you liked this book by reviewing it at your favorite retailer.

If you do write a review, please email me at rose@rosegarciabooks.com. I'd like to personally thank you.

Once again, thanks for reading *Final Death*! To stay in the know regarding my appearances and future releases, please subscribe to my newsletter at:

www.rosegarciabooks.com/download-finallife.

You'll also be able to access some deleted scenes from *Final Life* when you sign up! And for those active on social media, you can find all my social media links at the bottom of each page of my website:

www.rosegarciabooks.com.

I'd love to stay in touch!

Coming soon... a new trilogy sure to thrill fans of *Ender's Game*, *The Maze Runner*, and *The Giver*. Stay tuned!

ABOUT THE AUTHOR

Rose Garcia is a lawyer turned writer who's always been fascinated by science fiction and fantasy. From a very young age, she often had her nose buried in books about other-worlds, fantastical creatures, and life and death situations. More recently she's been intrigued by a blend of science fiction and reality, and the idea that some supernatural events are, indeed, very real. Fueled by her imagination, she created The Transhuman Chronicles—a series of books about people who have overcome human limitations. Rose lives in Houston with her husband and two kids. You can visit Rose at: www.rosegarciabooks.com

Made in the USA
San Bernardino, CA
27 April 2017